THE
MORRIGAN CHRONICLES
AWAKENING

N.A. MONTGOMERY

This is a work of fiction. Names, characters and places are a product of the
author's imagination and are used fictitiously.

I have had countless support from my friends, family and professional team that have helped me launch this new book. My three children are my life and their energy drives me daily. I cannot thank each of you enough. But, this book is dedicated to my Mom & Dad. Your guidance and belief in me gives me courage. Mom — this one's for you.

CHAPTER 1

I SLEPT MORE soundly than ever in my eight hundred and thirty-nine years. I was warm, comfortable, carefree and safe. My entire life, once I came of age, has been as a warrior for the Tuatha de Danann. These feelings of security were mostly foreign to me.

The distant sound of a horn stirred me. Familiar, but still I stayed rooted in slumber, unable to move. Not wanting to move. A second sounding of the horn and I had the gnawing feeling I should get up. There was something of importance in the sound, but I couldn't wake. I wouldn't wake. The third sounding of the horn and my eyes shot open. The horn from a white sacrificial bull blown three times. What was going on?

I stood and I drew both my swords in a single movement. The smell was of damp rotting earth mixed with stagnant air. My nose curled at the scent and the stale air held heavy, making it hard to breathe. There was a small light, the size of a pebble, the only light in total darkness. It began to grow though I hadn't moved. I looked around. My fellow Tuatha were around me, swords readied as well. My King to my left. None of us said a word. None of us moved.

Confusion took over my thoughts. I was in the middle of a great battle only a moment ago. Wasn't I? What had happened? The King looked to me, just as dumbfounded as I felt and spoke, "Morrigan?"

My eyes didn't leave the light as I whispered, "Be ready."

A silhouette walked into the center of the light though I couldn't make out the face, my eyes having trouble adjusting to the contrast from the darkness. The walk was familiar but nothing else. He wore unfamiliar clothes. Loose pants that went all the way to the ground in a shiny grey, a material I'd never seen. Sturdier than silk but flowing as he moved. He didn't wear boots but black shoes that wouldn't hold up for a day of walking across the countryside. His shirt was the crispest of white and a jacket over it matched his pants. He stopped and smiled. Recognition hit me.

I whispered the familiar man's name, "Emrys."

CHAPTER 2

EMRYS WALKED UP, towering over me at six foot five inches of solid muscle, dwarfing my five foot eight inch frame. I'm a slender yet strong woman and as always, his mass enveloped me. His thick chest and his arms spread wide, lifting me into a spin while holding me close. Tears streamed out of his soft grey eyes as he laughed.

He nuzzled my cheek, not bothering to pull my long red hair out of the way. I could feel the wetness of his tears against my skin. I knew they were tears of joy but my heart ached that he seemed so emotional. My truest friend. Our souls were intertwined in centuries of friendship and I could feel the relief that poured from him.

I pulled back to see his face though he loosened his embrace on me only slightly. His silver hair was cut short rather than the shoulder length he had worn what seemed to be a few minutes ago when we were in battle together. I ran my fingers over it, not liking the change and not understanding why it looked like this. His hair was like the metal silver, spun into soft strands and not that of an elderly human, though his solid build and lack of wrinkles would never allow him to be confused for an old man. The contrast of his bronze skin and grey eyes gave him a strange and appealing look at the same time.

"Emrys, why do you look like this and what is going on?" I said as the King cleared his throat next to me.

Emrys sat me down but still wore his grin. "King Conall." He bowed then continued, "There will be time to explain but it is not now. We must go through the Great Oak to a place of safety I have readied for us. There I will explain all that I know."

He grabbed my hand, barely taking his eyes off me to lead us out. My hand felt at home in his. We walked in silence only because my head spun with so many questions I didn't know where to begin. We made our way into the morning light, the sun barely above the horizon. There stood a man with the sacred horn and the Stone of Fal, one of the four treasures from our home.

CHAPTER 3

KING CONALL LOOKED at Emrys. Being King he was naturally imposing, even to a great Druid such as Emrys. The King's patience—though Emrys said there would be an explanation—was dwindling, seeing the man with one of our treasures and the bull's horn.

Emrys couldn't let go of his grin but seeing the seriousness of the King's expression he raised his hands. "Please, we are but a short walk to one of the Great Oaks, and it will lead us to a place of safety. We will have quite a walk once we pass through. I'll explain everything on the way."

The man holding the horn stared at me. He was human, that much I could tell. His fears were not masked as ours surely were.

Emrys picked up the Stone of Fal, took the horn from the man's hands, and led the way. The air was cool and pure, if not a little damp from the fog. The emerald green of the grass on the rolling hills held the dew. At least the familiar landscape was comforting to me.

Emrys strode next to the human. "Come, boy, I'll explain to you, too. Bet you didn't think you were going to see three hundred Tuatha de Danann come walking out of a mound of dirt when you woke up this morning, did you?"

The man, obviously stunned, stuttered and sounded out as best he could, "Thoo-a-day Du-non?"

Emrys let out his hearty laugh, "Yes, I suppose you need some catching up as well. Seems like I'm the only one around here who knows what is going on. Patience, boy."

"Quit calling me boy!" he shouted and planted his feet.

Anger replaced the fear on his face. Or more likely the anger was a result of the fear. That I could relate to. "I am twenty-eight years old. I'm a grown man, and my name is Neil. You and everyone here look to be a few years younger than me, so stop with calling me boy."

A soft chuckle erupted from us, which only seemed to anger him more. Emrys' face was soft and friendly even after the outburst. "Relax, young thundercat."

Before Neil could protest any more, Emrys stopped in front of the Great Oak. The only tree in the sea of hills.

"Neil," he said, dripping in a most patronizing tone. "This is a Great Oak. One that is very old, containing great magic, and is friendly to us. These people and myself are supernaturals. We can use Great Oaks as a sort of portal. We can enter into one and come out through another Great Oak at another location. Anywhere in the world. Humans cannot. At least not without the help of a supernatural."

Neil stood looking at Emrys as if he'd sprouted a second head.

Emrys saw the man was slow to catch on. "Frak it, follow me." And with that he grabbed the man and stepped through the tree.

We followed Emrys. I was first, followed by the King. Before stepping through I looked back. Emrys was right, there were about three hundred of us. Three hundred. We were more like three thousand strong when we began the battle this morning. Did we really have so many casualties? I was at the center of the battle and couldn't see beyond what was in front of me. Slashing and taking heads, that was all that I focused on.

Emrys and Neil stood back a few feet as I exited. Taking in the landscape, I could see we were in a thick forest of trees. I did as Emrys had, stepping aside so that others could follow through, the King stepping with me.

"Have you seen Treasach, Alastar and Aine?" I asked, no formality in my voice for the King. Perhaps a hint of the panic I felt welling inside me. His blue eyes took me in.

"Ease yourself, Morrigan. You were so preoccupied that you didn't notice my children were beside me. They are safe." Then he couldn't help himself and winked. "As is my mate." King Conall smiled and the next to walk through the Great Oak was Treasach.

Like his father, Treasach was tall and handsome. Not as tall as Emrys but only a few inches shorter. Tuatha hair was either golden, red or somewhere in between, but his was as gold as sunshine. That is exactly what I thought of when I looked at either of them—sunshine. His skin was bronzed and his turquoise eyes stood out in contrast. The dark brown leather pants and vests that we wore in battle complimented his coloring. As he stood next to the King I couldn't help thinking how alike they looked. All but the eyes. The King had the same hair and skin but his eyes were a deep blue. The color of the ocean I once saw from a beach covered with sand.

Alastar and Aine were next to come through. The twins. Alastar, like his father and older brother, wore the brown battle gear, but his stockier stature made it look like his muscles would burst through the leather. Treasach was tall and powerful but moved with finesse and sleekness. Alastar was straight brute force and looked it. He was the deadliest of the three in battle. His eyes matched his father's but he had an added twinkle in them that revealed a great heart and usually a little mischief.

Aine, like her twin brother Alastar, had bright red hair. While his was shoulder length and pulled back, hers flowed down to her lower back even when braided. In my opinion, she was the most beautiful of all the Tuatha. She was tall and agile. Strong yet fragile. Fiery hair and cool turquoise eyes. Everything about her contradictory, at times even her mood.

The King's mate, Deidra, came next. Not one of my favorites, but even I couldn't deny she was poised, beautiful and usually very kind, though I could unnerve her at times. Her hair was a blonde so pale that it was platinum rather than the usual warmer colors of our people. Unlike most of us, her skin shimmered silver rather than gold. Her eyes were the palest of blue. Everything about her look was cool. She radiated femininity. She walked as though she floated, stopping next to the King, giving me a regal nod.

I lifted my chin to her. Not very polite, but at least I acknowledged her presence. That was the best I could offer. Treasach just winked at me.

Coming through the Great Oak single file took quite a while so I went to Emrys. He was speaking to Neil. Glancing at me, he wound his hand in mine and I pressed up against him. Wherever we were it was cooler than I was used to and his warmth comforted me.

His baritone voice was smooth like black velvet though I suspected he had magic laced into the words to keep Neil calm as he spoke. "I am a Druid, and as such I am a great conductor of magic."

Neil broke free of the calming magic. "Emrys—as in Merlin? Like King Arthur and Merlin?"

Emrys rolled his eyes. "For crying out loud, my name is Emrys. I've never gone by Merlin and whatever pile of demon crap you have read in the stories about King Arthur, forget all of it. You'll soon learn the real story, and the first lesson is that my name is not Merlin. Nor am I an old wizard who wears a pointy hat. Never have and never will."

I had no idea what he was talking about. And why would someone think his name is Merlin? It sounds like a girl's name. And what does a pointy hat have to do with anything?

"As I was saying…" Emrys' words thickened with magic, "I'm a Druid. Like the Tuatha, and all supernaturals, we cease aging once we reach our maximum growth. Approximately age twenty-five to twenty-seven. We do not die of old age."

"You're all immortal?" Neil blurted.

"No!" Emrys' patience was now being tested. "Nothing is immortal. We die like anything that lives. We do not age. Now as I said, I'm a Druid. Magic is my strength, and all you need to know is that I'm damn good at it."

He paused but Neil stayed quiet, waiting to hear more.

"These fine folks are the Tuatha de Danann. They are from the four great cities: Falias, Goirias, Findias and Muirias. They are warriors that the Creator made to balance out great evil."

"The Creator… you mean God?" Neil couldn't help himself this time.

Emrys' look was patient and I could see why he was the great Druid leader. "As I said, you need to unlearn most things that you know. The answer is yes and no. Yes, the Creator is the God that you worship. He is *the* God. He created everything. He created the Earth, the waters, the animals and humans. He then created his children, the lesser Gods, to help rule. To break it down for you kid, he's the boss but he needed to delegate. So now you have the Creator's offspring helping things along and as things go, there's always some bad and some good. Just like any other creatures, jealousy and fighting erupted among the Gods. Resentment. They wanted the Earth for themselves. The bad Gods began wreaking havoc on the humans. Even taking some and twisting them into creatures to cause more destruction. The Gods are siblings and are bound not to harm one another. So, he created the Tuatha to fight the evil on land and the Fomoire to fight the evil of the seas."

"We are all through," shouted Brian, my second in command.

King Conall imposed himself on Emrys. "Where are we headed?"

"As you can see, we are in a thick forest," Emrys began. "I have set us up in a place about five miles from here, so we have a bit of a walk."

"Good." the King kept a close eye on Emrys. "Now you can fill me in on what is going on."

"Yes, of course," Emrys agreed. I couldn't help but smile that he didn't call the King 'Sire' or 'Your Highness' as we would. Being a Druid, he wasn't a subject and Emrys always made it clear that he worked *with* us and not *for* us. Another reason I adored him.

Neil was impatient to get on with the story Emrys had begun. "So if the Creator—"

Neil was cut off as King Conall picked him up by the collar of his shirt. The always calm look on his face contrasted with what I knew he felt. He kept his voice steady yet stern. "Emrys, I don't know who this is, but you will tell us what is going on now."

He threw Neil to the ground and his gaze hardened on Emrys. Typical Emrys looked unworried and fiddled with a fingernail.

He helped Neil to his feet then turned to lead the way and we began to follow. A full minute stretched by before he spoke. His voice was soft, knowing that our hearing was far more acute than humans and we would all be able to hang on every word. "We were to battle Arwan, God of terror and revenge. Your cousins the Fomoire may have been your family and allies at one time but for centuries you have battled them. They, wanting to be rid of humans or at the very least control them, the Tuatha wanting to protect. They made an arrangement with Arwan that they would fight with him to defeat the Tuatha and not turn on him as long as he would leave the Fomoire alone and enslave the humans. What is the last thing you remember?"

King Conall smiled but knowing him as I did this was not a friendly gesture. This was a precursor to him losing his patience. His voice not betraying emotion he answered, "Our forces gathered as the sun rose over the hills at our backs. We faced the sea. Arthur and his Knights were behind us and the Druids behind them, ready to heal. The Fomoire appeared at the shore with Arwan cowardly standing behind them. We charged and met them in battle. We fought for hours, most of the day. The sun hung low in the sky looking to be swallowed by the sea when we began to make headway. Morrigan, yourself and Alastar fought in a fury, carving a path closer to Arwan. Myself, Arthur, and his Knight Gawain charged through. The three of us fought Arwan. The three of you held the Fomoire at bay. Arwan mostly battled with me, seeing Arthur and Gawain as weak. Arwan slashed Arthur's sword, breaking it in half. Then he slid his sword deep into Gawain's leg. Thinking them no threat he fought me with all his might. Arthur shouted for me to throw him my sword. Arwan was paying him no attention. I grabbed Gawain's sword to keep fighting and threw Arthur mine, knowing that the sword of the Tuatha would be the only one to defeat a God. Before Arwan could react, Arthur drove it deep into his body. Arwan stood frozen before Arthur pulled it out and then took the head of the evil bastard." The King paused, running his hand through his beard. "Then we awoke inside the Earth."

Neil's mouth hung open in amazement, but I had to give him credit, he said nothing this time. He stopped walking for a moment but continued on when I bumped into his shoulder. Yeah sure, I didn't need to do that but I couldn't help myself. It was colder than I was used to and though I was confused, I was in a hurry to get to shelter. Finding out what had happened next to a roaring fire and mug of ale sounded much better than hiking through this cold forest.

Emrys looked deep in thought. He kept his eyes ahead paying attention where he stepped, but the path was well beaten through the thick woods. The trees held no leaves and the wind had picked up. The whole forest and sky looked as if it had been washed in grey.

Clearing his throat he asked. "What do you know of Artaius?"

I was cold and my mood was darkening. I snapped, "Not a particularly powerful God. Mostly goes around causing trouble. He's like the pesky little brother with a twisted sense of humor."

Emrys nodded. "That's right. Kind of a punk. Turns out

he's not just the little moron we thought him to be. Remember Arthur's Queen, Guinevere?"

King Conall answered this time, his mood worse than mine. "We fought alongside Arthur and his Knights. We've never met her, but of course have heard her mentioned."

Emrys shook his head. "We should have."

Neil was now walking next to me. This close I noticed him to be about six foot tall. I hadn't paid him much attention until now. His eyes were warm like caramel and his short hair a dark rich brown. His face was kind. Sweet even. His eyes trusting. Though we looked to be the same age as he, our eyes didn't hold that kind of innocence.

Emrys finally broke his silence and brought my focus back to him. "Guinevere was not Guinevere."

"Artaius?" I asked but instantly knew. My gut wrenched. Something terrible had happened. Something bigger than any of us knew. I was piecing the puzzle together. It hit me before Emrys even told the story. He looked at me, slowly nodding. My suspicions were right. I fought to maintain a mask of confidence and calm. Glad that I had figured it out, having a head start to gather myself before Emrys spelled it out for everyone else.

"Yes," he continued. "Artaius had taken the form of a beautiful woman and seduced Arthur. Constantly whispering in his ear. Arthur had become a puppet and didn't know it. We didn't know it. Artaius convinced Arthur the Tuatha needed his help in defeating Arwan and the Fomoire but once that was done, the Tuatha planned to enslave all of mankind to serve them."

"That is absurd!" Deidra shrieked.

Leave it to the always proper one to be offended rather than looking at the big picture.

Emrys shrugged. "I know that, but Arthur was convinced. Artaius told Arthur that the battle needed to last as long as possible, so that there would be maximum Fomoire and Tuatha casualties. That both races were a threat to all of humanity. He needed to get the sword of the Tuatha at all costs. With it he could reign and have power over anyone or anything that stood before him. That he would rule over humanity and that the supernatural beings needed to be banished. All supernaturals."

He paused though no one asked any questions. I assume he was letting this information sink in. Convinced everyone had wrapped their minds around the tale, he pressed on. "Before the battle began, Artaius gave Arthur a single drop of his blood. It would bond them. The sword is the only weapon that can kill a God, and a God cannot wield it. King Conall willingly gave the sword to Arthur, technically making it his. The moment he struck Arwan down he summoned Artaius' power and banished all on the battlefield to sleep deep in the Mother Earth. The Druids saw this happening and hesitated in their confusion. Arthur ordered the Knights to take their heads."

Emrys' eyes filled with tears of pain, though he held them back. "The Knights whom the Druids healed, trained with, lived with, even loved, on orders of their King, struck every last one of them down... at least they thought they did. Gawain was stunned at the sudden turn of events and let Marisol and Deia escape."

All three hundred of us stopped in our tracks, not one of us able to move. It was as if a cold from deep inside iced over our veins, keeping us frozen in place. A sadness of this magnitude simply didn't get absorbed instantly. A slaughter of our friends, Tuatha and Druid alike, whom we had intertwined our lives with for centuries was going to soak in slowly and painfully. The pain we felt now would be nothing compared to what would come. Tears didn't fall. Not because we were stoic. We were just not able to believe it. I've had plenty of heartache and experienced many losses on the battlefield. This was unimaginable.

King Conall looked strong and regal. I knew him well and knew his heart ached but he held himself together for his people. He was acting. "Emrys, there are many more questions I have.

That I'm sure we all have. How long were we asleep, and where is my sword now?"

"I'm getting to that." Emrys began walking again. "We're almost to our shelter. Just over this ridge." We slowly followed, our minds not wanting to hear more but knowing we must. "Once the, uh, battle was over and the humans made their way back to Camelot, Gawain was disenchanted with Arthur and went to speak with him. He knew something was not right. Arthur told him that the Tuatha planned to enslave them but Gawain didn't believe him. He began to notice Guinevere spending more and more time with Arthur, never leaving his side. Arthur began planning a campaign to conquer all the surrounding kingdoms. Gawain tried reasoning with Arthur that this was not what Camelot stood for. That this was a time of peace. He knew Arthur would be unstoppable with the sword. He sought out Marisol and Deia whom he helped hide far to the north. They told him that he needed to steal the sword and get it to them. That they would send it to another realm where nobody would be able to reach it. He managed to get it one night as Arthur slept. He was to meet Marisol and Deia outside the castle walls. He miraculously made it out of the castle with over fifty arrows in his back. They grabbed him, the sword, and disappeared in the forest through a Great Oak. They still didn't know that Artaius was involved at this point. They were in the middle of healing Gawain when Guinevere, or Artaius as it were, showed up. Their power was weak from healing and they weren't able to fight Artaius off. Deia fell first and instead of using the last of her power to fight, Marisol sent the sword away, though nobody knows where. Artaius left Gawain to die. But he didn't… otherwise we wouldn't know this much."

We crested the ridge. This was the edge of the forest. Beyond lay an enormous lawn, crisp with frost that led to a… castle? No, it didn't look like a castle but it was as big as one. The structure was made out of red bricks and looked to be able to hold several hundred. There were so many windows—it seemed to have a window every few feet. Judging from the way they lined up the building had four levels. It was a marvel.

Next to it were the stables. It was made of brick as well, looking to be a smaller version of the lodging accommodations and opened up into a massive field with a beautiful white fence. I could see at least a dozen equines. We were going to need more in order to travel.

Our pace quickened, knowing that we could warm ourselves and get something to eat. The news that Emrys had brought had taken its toll on me and I'm sure everyone else. I grew wary not seeing any smoke coming from chimneys knowing it would be a while before the rooms would warm. Wait... where were the chimneys?

I've seen pyramid structures in a land of sand that stretched up to the sky. Great buildings of white with columns overlooking the sea, bluer than can be described. I've even seen large cats bigger than wolves in a forest of strange trees. This was something foreign.

"Emrys, I've never seen a building like this." My mind was trying to put the pieces together but unable to. "Where are we? Are we still in the Earthly realm?"

Emrys' uneasy look worried me but at least he answered. "We are far from Erin. If you were to look west and travel as far as the sea goes this is where you would be. You and I have been here before, Morrigan. Do you remember the people who wore leathers not unlike yours? They rode on small horses with no saddles and decorated their long black hair with feathers?"

"Yes, I remember. We tracked a pack of cannibal dwarves there. Nasty little things. They had eaten several of the people before we were able to take their heads," I said, recalling the trip. I didn't remember seeing anything like this while there, though.

Emrys nodded. "That's right. Well the land is vast. More so than you can imagine. We are in the middle of that land. A place called Missouri in the country known as The United States of America."

In the distance I saw a shiny black metal carriage with no horses pulling it fly down the path towards the house at a speed that no horse could match. The others saw it too and we all slid our swords from their sheaths.

"Calm down! Calm down! Everything is fine," Emrys boomed. "That is a mode of transportation, like a horse or a carriage. It's what is used now to travel."

We kept our swords drawn and King Conall asked what we were all thinking. "Used now? How long have we been sleeping, Emrys?"

Emrys didn't look at the King but at me. He didn't blink. I held my breath. All three hundred of us held our breaths. The seconds stretched. Finally he answered. "You were spelled and held under in sleep for... one thousand three hundred eighty-five years. It is now the year 2017."

CHAPTER 4

ONE THOUSAND THREE hundred and eighty-five years. I had trouble grasping everything Emrys had told us but managed to hold myself together. The loss of so many. Us ultimately losing the battle we had fought. I even knew that we had been spelled into sleep but I thought it to be no more than a year or two. I could even accept ten. A hundred. One thousand three hundred and eighty-five years. I was no longer cold and hungry. I felt nothing. I was numb. I don't know how long I stood like that. Nausea hit me as my head spun out of control, dropping me to my knees. I couldn't panic in front of our people. I just needed to get my wits about me.

Warm hands gingerly touched my shoulders and helped me up. "Put your sword away and let's get inside," Neil said softly.

I looked at King Conall. He had his hands intertwined with Deidra's. Gross. One more thing I had to endure on this damned day. His eyes met mine. I stiffened and put on the bravest face I could muster and nodded to him.

"Emrys, lead us into the shelter," King Conall ordered.

We followed Emrys, not saying a word. There was no digesting this kind of information. You just had to sit there and wait, hoping that it would eventually make sense. One foot moved in front of another but I don't know how. I felt hollow. Not paying attention, I stumbled on a rock. Neil caught my elbow and waist to keep me from toppling over. I grabbed his arm to steady myself. I kept walking for who knows how long and realized I was still holding his arm. I didn't care. I felt that if I let go the world would spin so fast I'd fly off of it.

We were close to the lodging when Emrys stopped, turning to us. "There's more to discuss but for now let's get you settled. There are humans here that are on our side. I've gathered the bravest descendants of the Knights and the half-breed Druids I could find. We are not alone."

Emrys stopped speaking aloud and began speaking to us in our minds, something he didn't do very often. Only in times of great signifigance. "Tuatha de Danann hold strong. The Knights are human and the Druids I've gathered are the bastard children that were half Druid half human. Their Druid blood was diluted even more through time. They have pledged to help us and I believe them. As Gawain risked his life to do what was right I know there is great good in humanity. But, this would not be the first time we were betrayed. They are unaware of your strength and skill. Nor do they know much about you. You are of myth and legend to them. Do not fully trust them. I've told them you have a powerful King and are supernatural warriors forged by the Creator himself to fight the evils of the world. That is all that they know. Give them no more information about yourselves or me. We do not know what details could come back to haunt us."

We made our way inside. I saw no fireplace but instantly felt warm. The scent of vanilla wafted faintly through the air. The floor was marble with thick rugs running down the center and the walls a highly polished dark wood. It was beautiful.

We entered into a large open hall. Long wooden tables with benches, enough to seat hundreds, filled the room. At the back table in the center sat another one of our treasures. The Cauldron of Dagda. The cauldron ensured that whomever ate from it never left wanting more. It supplied an endless amount of food. My eyes misted at the sight of it. Not because I knew my hunger would be satiated, but because it was a familiar sight. It represented home. A home that no longer existed, at least not one that I knew anymore.

We ate our fill. Afterwards, we were shown our living quarters, each of us with our own room. King Conall, Emrys and I met in what he called the library. The sun had long set but glass globes placed in the ceiling and on poles glowed bright. I preferred the candles I was used to, accompanied by a fire in a hearth. As long as I could remember I always found the warmth and flickering of the light comforting. This light felt harsh. Books lined the walls, floor to ceiling. A large desk at one end with a metal box on it. There were eight leather chairs surrounding a round table in the center of the room where we took seats.

King Conall wasted no time. "Emrys, explain to me how you were spelled to sleep along with us and yet you escaped."

As a Teulu I am a King's bodyguard. There are twelve of us. We are the most skilled in battle. Thankfully, after the massive losses we incurred, we at least had survived. I am the leader of the Teulu and always accompany the King in important matters. I was numb from the day's events and felt ridiculous for not having thought the question myself. I guess that is why I am not King.

Emrys mirrored King Conall's urgency in answering. "I was awakened ninety-seven years ago. I am unsure why or how. It was as it was with you. The Earth opened up and I saw all the Tuatha sleeping. I poured every ounce of my magic into trying to wake you, but nothing happened. I walked out and the Earth instantly closed. There was a leatherbound book encased in glass with Gawain's letter telling of what had happened."

Emrys rose and walked over to a shelf, lifting a glass case and bringing it to us. He opened the case and removed the book. Opening it, he slid out a piece that was unbound and handed it to us. I moved closer to the King so I could read it as well. I had to focus on not getting sidetracked by King Conall's scent. Musk, Earth... man.

"This is the letter that was lying on top of the book when I came out. Read it for yourself."

With all the Druids gone I have no way to break the sleeping spell the Tuatha de Danann are under. I hope that by awakening the Mighty Emrys, Lord of all the Druids, you are able to break the spell and restore balance to the world, for evil outweighs good immensely at the moment and I fear all is lost.

Seek out Druantia, Queen of the Druids, Lady of the Lake, safe in the realm between twilight and night. She will give guidance where I have none.

She will lead you to me when the time comes. You will know I am friend when I speak the words, "Long lost friend. Long lost enemy. I am nothing more than a memory."

What in the hell did that mean?

King Conall spoke my thought aloud. We were always in sync with one another. Well most of the time.

"Frak if I know." Emrys rubbed his temples. I forgot how stressful this had been on him as well. I would need to check in on him later.

"Next question." King Conall was on point and down to business. "What does Neil have to do with this?"

Great question, King. Again, I was so behind playing catch up that I'd lost all reasoning, it seemed.

Emrys took a long drink of water. "Getting to that. I planned to do what the note suggested. Getting to the land between twilight and night is not easy, though. It can only be entered on Samhain. It is now called Halloween. It is the day that our two realms are closest to one another. I assume whomever woke me knew that and did so the day before. When you enter on Samhain, regardless how long it may seem that you are there, minutes even, you come out on the following Samhain. One year.

I entered the other realm and was met by Queen of the Druids, Druantia. Lady of the Lake. I am not ashamed to say I was terrified at being alone and lost for what to do. I wept, and wept hard. She soothed me and told me that not all was lost. That there was still hope. How I was awakened was clouded to her. She was unable to see how it was done and that if she could not see, it must have been by a great magic. My quest was to attain the Stone of Fal. The true King of Erin, which would have to be a descendent of Arthur, would scream when he stood upon it. Once I had the true King, he could blow on the sacred horn of a sacrificed white bull that would awaken the Tuatha."

Emrys took a bottle and poured a red liquid, wine, into a glass for each of us.

"Here," he handed them to us. "This has been a great day for me. I know you are grieving and still trying to grasp everything that I've told you but I've had almost a hundred years to cope. I've been a hundred years without my family though, and I feel like celebrating."

King Conall smiled and took a drink, as did I. The King softened and nodded. "Emrys, I am eternally grateful to you for awaking our people. Did Druantia say what needs to be done or how we are to defeat Artaius?"

Nodding, Emrys continued. "She told me that I would need a great fortress, to gather the descendants of the Knights and Druids and that once the Tuatha arrived they would help train them for the great battle. But that it would still not be enough. We need to retrieve the sacred sword. The sword is the only weapon that can defeat Artaius. We just need to find the sword and have Neil formally *give* it back to you."

I cut Emrys off. "The sword was sent to another realm. Do you know where?"

This time shaking his head, he expounded on the story. "No, I do not, but Druantia said that once I awaked you I was to bring Morrigan with me. She promised by that time she would have the information on where it is and how to get it."

Finally I felt like I had my wits back with me. "You said we could only enter the land between twilight and night on Samhain. How long until then?"

"Almost a year's time. It is now December." Emrys answered. But December meant nothing to me and I could tell he knew by my face.

Emrys sighed. "You know how we have the gift of communication? How we have always been able to enter a Great Oak and travel all over the entire Earth and even though we don't speak the native languages of the people we come into contact with, we can understand them and they can understand us?"

"Of course." I took another sip of the wine, noting how warm I felt inside.

He grinned at me and then at King Conall. "My friends, it has been a very long time and the world has changed much. So much that I fear you would not recognize it. We cannot get bogged down by such things, we have a large task before us. With your permission, I shall cast a spell tonight that when all Tuatha awake in the morning they will understand the workings of this world. A sort of—catch you up on the past thousand or so years."

The King gave a weary smile. The day had taken its toll. "That would be fine, Emrys. Can you by chance include some comfort in that spell? I worry about my people."

"I cannot take grief away, but I can offer hope. And the smallest spark of hope is all that we need in these great times of darkness," he said as he stood and bowed. Emrys must have been in an excellent mood to show the King this level of respect.

CHAPTER 5

I SAT UP in the bed, pushing the soft blankets back. A white down comforter and matching thousand thread count Egyptian cotton sheets. I shook my head, astonished that I knew that. Emrys never ceases to amaze me.

Making my way to the bathroom I turned the water on for a hot shower. Understanding and knowing about the new advances still couldn't keep me from marveling at them. It's the difference between knowing unicorns are real and actually seeing one for the first time. Amazing. The bathing experience was wonderful. Honeysuckle body soap with a loofah. Loofah, what a funny word. Shampoo and conditioner scented of flowers I've never smelled. Lotion that made my skin as soft as my hair. It was luxurious.

Clean and dry, I stood naked in front of a full-length mirror. I had rarely seen my reflection before. I am able to command magic somewhat, but I've only seen myself a few times, and never my entire self. I walked over to the closet knowing there would be clothes in there. I went through each item: jeans, dresses, sweaters and blouses. There were enough clothes and shoes in this closet for ten women. I decided to put my leathers back on.

Lacing up my boots, I felt myself again. Strapping on all my sheaths I secured my assortment of knives and swords. A dagger in each boot, medium swords crossed on my back and my long sword down the center. The hilts of my swords fanned out behind my head. My long red hair hung over one shoulder, almost to my navel. Using the smallest hint of magic, with a flick of my wrists, the hair went up into an ornate braid that circled my head.

My stomach grumbled, reminding me of my hunger, when there was a knock at my door.

"It's me, beautiful," the voice came through the thick wood.

Opening the door, I saw my Emrys with his wide warm smile. He couldn't help but tease me. "My, my, my you are an image to behold. Your beauty is the kind that men write poems about. That countries go to battle over. That…"

I rolled my eyes. "Keep it up and I'll make you marry me."

"Oh, hell no. I don't know what you do to men but I've seen the aftermath. I want no part of that." He laughed, smacking me on the back.

I grabbed him in a hug and couldn't let go. "Oh Emrys, I'm so glad you're here. I couldn't make it through this without you. I'm so sorry you had to be alone for so long."

I pulled my head away, not letting go to see his face. He smiled and kissed the top of my head. "Morrigan, I clung to this day. I knew I'd find a way, and that I'd see you again. That's how I made it through. That's how I know we will make it through this next set of trials. We ain't letting these fools take us down."

I understood this vernacular was more in line with the times but it made me smile nonetheless.

Treasach, Alastar and Aine walked in. I released Emrys and grabbed all three at once, pulling them to me. "I love you all so, so much. You know that, right?"

We clung to one another for several minutes and finally Alastar pulled away, giving me that twinkle in his eye. "Oh no, what did you do now? Are you getting banished already?"

Laughter filled the room. The kind that came from the heart. That filled the heart. Its warmth permeated throughout. I savored the moment, reminding myself to treasure this and remember it in darker times that would surely come.

Treasach leaned down, kissing my cheek. "Father wants to meet with you and the Teulu in the library in an hour. Nine o'clock sharp. Apparently we begin training the humans today."

"We just got here. I don't know why we can't spend a day getting accustomed," Aine chimed in.

"Your father is right," I said, wiping a stray hair from her face. "The sooner we begin, the better. Besides, staying busy will do us all some good."

"Well whatever we're doing, I can't do it on an empty stomach. Let's eat!" Alastar said, already walking out the door. That boy is always hungry.

We ate and chatted through breakfast noting that the Tuatha sat on one side of the large dining hall as the humans sat on the other. They stared in wonderment. We barely paid them any attention. I did notice Neil sitting off from the rest looking only at his food.

"Emrys." I threw a piece of potato at him to get his attention. "Neil is going to lead the humans. Why he is sitting apart? He looks left out. As their leader shouldn't they be clamoring for his attention?"

"Doesn't know them, I suppose. And they don't know him." Emrys threw the potato back at me. "I uh, well uh, he was in South Dakota, of all places when I found him. On his way to work, I believe. An attorney. I verified who he was and spelled him. He didn't really 'come to' so to speak, until after he blew the sacred horn three times."

We stared at him. "Are you fraking kidding me?" I couldn't help but laugh. "Poor kid. He's got to be the most confused person here."

I took another bite of fried potatoes and onions. "Think he's up for this?"

Emrys grinned. "That's your job, dearie. You are charged to make damn well sure he's ready for it."

I stopped chewing. Emrys, Treasach, Alastar and Aine laughed hysterically. I'm a great warrior and I trained all three of the King's children. They can attest, I am not known for my patience. Training Tuatha is one thing. Training a human, a human that has never been in battle, hell—probably not even a fight, was already grating my nerves.

Treasach wiped the tears of laughter from his eyes. "Better get to the library. Don't want the King pissed at you."

I put a string of curse words together so foul that even the furthest sitting Tuatha turned to look at me in shock. I was not known for manners or etiquette but I shocked even myself at my level of crudeness.

The King's children laughed harder at my insults as Emrys and I rose and headed for the library.

We made our way into the large room where the other Teulu had already gathered. Figures, wouldn't want to offend the King by being late. I shut the door behind me as the clock finished striking nine. Right on time... barely. My own mini-defiance at being tasked to train Neil. I'm not fond of humans and didn't like nor trust them when we fought alongside Arthur and his Knights. As it turned out, my instincts were right.

The King commanded the room. I've been on his good side and his bad many, many times. No matter what side of the line I was on with him he always trusted me, and I him. I trust him with my life and would give my life to save him. That said, I've been tempted to rip his head off a few times and today was one of them. I made my way to his side and stared blankly ahead as he spoke.

"My fellow Tuatha, we must first give thanks to Emrys. He has gone to great lengths to awaken us and provide us with such a fine place to reside and train. We begin training today. Emrys will begin training the Druid descendants. They will be but a shadow of the Druids that we called friends. That we called family. But they have Druid blood nonetheless, and will be able to help. It is upon him to get them as strong as they can be. Each of you and the warriors under you will begin training a group of humans. It is your responsibility to have them skilled in hand-to-hand combat and swordsmanship. The modern weapons will do nothing against the foes we face. Taking heads is always assured. These are not skills that they are familiar with, so begin with the very basics. Morrigan is tasked with training Neil and Neil alone. He needs to be ready to lead the Knights and command them. He is the true King of Erin and there is power in that. We have about one year until Samhain, which is when Emrys and Morrigan will travel to the land between twilight and night. Once there, they will be in that realm for one year. In that time, Brian will take over Neil's training and James will continue overseeing the training of the humans. By that time, Emrys, you will need to appoint the strongest of the Druids to oversee the training in your absence. That gives us two years total to get the humans we have ready for battle. You have your orders."

The King signaled that this was the end of our gathering by raising his head higher and stiffening his spine. This also signaled that there were to be no questions. Only obedience. We began to file out, me last. I cut my eyes to his, the turquoise color laced with fire when he finally met mine. He gave me an impish grin and softened his face. He whispered, "Morrigan... please."

And that's all it took to melt me. "Of course, my King."

CHAPTER 6

The other Tuatha and their human trainees were in a large facility attached to the residence. The Druids were in another. I wasn't sure what I had to work with in Neil and I needed the humans to follow him. If he was unimpressive I couldn't have the others seeing it. So I had one of my warriors tell him to meet me in the stables. There was an indoor arena that would do just fine. We would be training alone.

He walked in wearing leathers and boots similar to mine but black. These would be the clothes he would battle in. The leather was spelled to withstand claws, teeth, and any sharp weapon. I could tell by his stride that he was trying to project confidence but was unsure of himself.

"I had on gym clothes but the guy you sent to tell me to come here told me to wear this." He pulled at the leather vest. I couldn't help but notice his shoulders and biceps were more developed than I realized.

"We train in what we battle in," I managed to eke out semi-stoically.

"Okay. So where do we begin?" He smiled warmly, his caramel eyes trained on mine.

"We'll start with a five mile run and begin increasing distance when you can manage a quick pace. I need your endurance to be optimal. Let's get through that and when we get back we can begin hand-to-hand combat training."

"All right but I'll warn you, I lift weights in the gym regularly, but I've never been one to do much cardio. I'll do my best but I've never run five miles in my life."

I reassured him, "You are a descendant of Arthur. His blood runs through yours. There's strength in that. You will find yourself able to do more physically than you can imagine. You will be stronger, faster and more skilled than the rest. It's my job to help you get there."

We set off at a decent pace. One mile in and he seemed to be doing fine. I picked the pace up to a seven minute mile and he hung in. I decided to see how well he could do. If he would be able to hold this pace talking or if he would start gasping for air.

"So tell me about yourself, Neil."

He glanced over at me. It was cold out and though he had sweat on his face he had no problem answering. "In comparison to the past day, my life has been fairly ordinary. I grew up in a small town in South Dakota. Went to college at the University of Nebraska, then law school. Got a job at a firm in Lincoln. My dad passed away from a heart attack so I moved back to take care of my mom. Got a job as a prosecutor in a nearby town. Couple years later my mom passed away. I think it was from a broken heart. She died in her sleep. She was lost without my dad."

He never gasped for a single breath and his gaze stared off in the distance. His eyes were still warm but I could see the sadness. I know that sadness. Many of my loved ones have died in battle. Never of disease or old age, and I was blessed to have had them for very long periods of time. My heart ached for him.

"Anyway, I've spent the last year just working. I was actually contemplating a change. With my family gone there was no need for me to stay in South Dakota. Guess I got my wish." He laughed and smiled at me. I was glad it was cold out and that I had an excuse for the blush I know rose in my cheeks.

"What about you? Are your parents here?"

My turn. I guess I asked for this in opening a conversation. I kicked myself for ending up having to talk about myself. "No. They're not here. My parents died in battle a long time ago."

"I'm sorry." He looked embarrassed.

"Don't be. They lived for several hundred years." It was now my turn to stare off in the distance, remembering them.

"What were they like?" His voice pulled me back.

How much to divulge? I pondered. "My father was King. Ruler of the Tuatha. He was strong. Ruthless to his enemies and loving to his family and people. My mother was what a queen should be. Regal, beautiful, strong and a hell of a swordsman."

He laughed. "So you're a princess?"

Now it was my turn to laugh. "No, I'm not a princess."

"So is King Conall your brother?"

I choked and laughed. "No!"

"I just thought since he's King and your dad was King…"

I was still laughing. "Strong bloodlines breed strong Tuatha. The strength of our ancestors is passed down, but to be the ruler of our people is not decided by blood. You remember the Stone of Fal and how it sang when you stood upon it?"

"Barely. I was kind of in a trance." He laughed but I knew he spoke the truth.

"Well, that signaled you were the true King of Erin. That cannot be debated. We have a spear that is similar. We do not vote for our leader and politics do not come into play. The Spear of Lug is one of our sacred gifts and determines our King. When my father died, Conall was chosen."

What was I doing? I don't care for humans. King Conall and Emrys determined we were to tell the humans as little as possible and here I was spouting out information. I couldn't help myself.

I picked up the pace. A six minute mile pace to be exact. He held but I could tell he had to work at it. Good. Hopefully that would grind the talking to a halt.

The last quarter mile I slowed down to a walk. "And that was our warm up." I smiled seeing that he was still upright. The hard work was yet to come.

"So Morrigan, I'm going to be completely honest. I'll work my hardest and learn as much as I can but I'm not confident about any of this. I still can't completely wrap my head around it."

I didn't let my face betray any thoughts or doubts. My lungs had adapted to the frigid air and the cold felt good against my face. Judging by the dark clouds, snow would soon fall. I loved every season, but winter always was a welcome time of year for me. I could smell a fire burning off in the distance. A bonfire no doubt, to gather around between lessons.

"Neil," I began in as supporting a tone I could offer, "we have plenty of time, and I'm tasked solely with making sure you're ready. Don't worry. I give my word that you will physically and mentally be ready and we will prevail. I have no doubt of that."

I knew I sounded confident and I could tell by his expression that he believed every word. I wished I did. But knowing that building his confidence was crucial, I began laying that foundation. He would not come close to surviving if he had any doubts in himself.

Making our way into the stables I paused to pet a beautiful black gelding. He was massive and majestic.

"He likes you." I felt Neil's warm breath on the back of my neck.

Though it was invisible I brushed it off with my hand. "It's not that he likes me. He respects me. All animals have a pecking order. A difficult horse is just testing to see if you are below or above him."

I stepped away before turning to face him. "We'll begin with some basic hand-to-hand defensive moves. After lunch we'll begin attack strategies."

"You're the boss. Not that I'm doubting you, but aren't I supposed to learn how to use a sword?"

Having only trained Tuatha I was not accustomed to being questioned. "Footwork and strategy are the basics, and before you can even think of picking up a sword you need to at least become mediocre at the basics."

"Thanks for the vote of confidence." Sarcasm laced his words but he grinned, softening my prickly surface.

I circled him, my eyes evaluating every inch. "I would say 'master' the basics but I fear my definition of mastering something is very high and time is of the essence."

His eyes locked on mine and I stopped with my left profile in front of him. I telegraphed a right cross and he clumsily stumbled out of the way. "Sloppy, but your instincts are good and you managed to avoid contact."

"Then show me how to not do it sloppily." His face was genuine and open. No ego, no animosity. He was malleable and willing to let me mold him. Him trusting me was crucial for his success. Our success.

I walked behind him, placing my hand on his hips. "I want you to keep your feet flat on the ground, but shift your weight to your toes." I kept my hands where they were and could feel the shift. "Good, just like that. You always have your weight there. And by always I mean *always*. You've had twenty-eight years to relax back on your heels. That time is over. There is no time that you're relaxed now. Always on your toes."

He looked back over his shoulder at me. "I understand."

"Good," I said. "Your power comes from here." I used my hands on his hips to swivel them slightly until he mimicked the movement on his own. "Your hips and core will help you to move quicker, block impossibly hard hits, and attack with accuracy and strength."

I released my hands and walked in front of him. We began slowly, with me showing where I would punch or kick him and then showing him the appropriate block. I was impressed at how quickly he learned. His movements were becoming more and more fluid.

Several hours passed and I felt my hunger growing. "Let's take a break and get some lunch."

Neil rubbed the front of his left shoulder and nodded. "Good, I could use a break."

Before he could finish speaking I moved his hand away from his shoulder and felt it. Thick solid muscle enlarged from use. I used my thumb to press into the spot where the front shoulder muscle attached to the bone and he winced slightly. "It's inflamed a little. Ice it while we eat and make sure to tonight as well."

I still had my hands on his shoulder and that awkward moment of realizing I was close to him hit me. The warmness of his eyes held me there longer than I meant to stay. Pulling away, I turned to leave, breaking the moment.

"How's it going?" Emrys said, strolling towards me. I could see by the smirk on his face he had witnessed what had just happened and the warmth from my cheeks betrayed every word out of my mouth.

"We're just getting started, you needn't worry," I snipped.

I walked past him and never looked back.

I ate quickly and mostly listened to others talk but didn't add much to the conversation. The dining hall was full and today the energy buzzed with excitement. Tuatha, Druids and Knight descendants were intermixed in their seating. Laughter and camaraderie filled the room. Neil sat next to me and mostly spoke to Treasach. They laughed a few times at my expense, comparing the horrible training experiences I'd subjected them to.

I raised my eyebrow as Treasach rose, he kissed the top of my head then winked at Neil. "Listen to her and you'll have nothing to worry about. She trained me. She's the best." Then he headed off.

"The King's children love you," Neil said as a statement, not a question.

"And I love them with all of my heart," I replied. "Time to practice attacking, so finish up."

We went back to the stables and practiced until evening, followed by dinner with everyone else. We stuck to this schedule for two months. Run in the morning. Defensive training before lunch, attack training after and then dinner. My evenings were spent with Emrys and the King debriefing them on how the day went.

CHAPTER 7

THE PAST TWO months had been grueling. Physically Neil did great, but I could tell the monotony and constant training was mentally draining him.

We chatted with the King's children throughout breakfast. Neil sat on one side of me and Emrys on the other while the children sat opposite of us. Emrys always liked to stir up whatever he could to cause someone embarrassment. Today he was directing his mischief towards Alastar, the strongest of the three and ornery in his own right. I loved when Emrys picked on him because it would end with Alastar chasing him and Emrys barely escaping. Tears streamed down my face as I laughed when Emrys tripped over Aine's foot that had suddenly shot out and Alastar began giving him a noogie.

I slapped my hand on Neil's back. "Come on, let's head to the stables. I have a surprise for you today."

Neil had been the perfect student the past couple of months. He was true to his word. He'd listened, practiced, and given his full effort every single day. I respected that in him.

The jovial mood from breakfast still held in my heart and I cupped my hands over his eyes as we walked into the arena. I kept stumbling on his heels, walking so close behind with my arms around his head, giggling at my own clumsiness.

I could feel his cheeks rise in a smile as he spoke. "I sure hope you got me new boots, because you've probably ruined mine stepping on my feet this much."

"Even better, I promise," I whispered into his ear.

"Keep your eyes closed," I said, almost singing, releasing my hands. I grabbed his hands and placed my gift into them. He held the gift and I knew he recognized what it was but he held on to my hand. Softly stroking the back of it.

My heart raced at his touch. It annoyed me a couple of months ago that he had this effect on me but now I smiled at giving in to it. I stared at him. His eyes remained closed. His hand was wrapped around mine. My breath was tight in my chest. My anticipation of giving Neil the gift mixed with his touch made my emotions swirl.

Gathering every ounce of composure I had while suppressing the rush of hormones, I took his hand that held mind and wrapped it around his gift. "Okay... open."

His caramel eyes held mine. His hands held the sword that was his gift. He didn't look away from me.

Though I liked the intensity of his look, worry grew in the pit of my stomach that maybe he didn't like the sword or care about it. "I personally forged that sword. I made it for you."

Still looking deep into my eyes he didn't hesitate. "Absolutely beautiful. What's not to love?"

I had to lighten the mood, and do it quickly. The intensity of what I felt, what I knew he felt, needed to be put aside... for now at least. "You haven't even looked at it," I chided.

His warm genuine smile shattered any doubt I had as he finally shifted his gaze from me to the sword. "The sword is beautiful, too. And I love it." He paused to look up and gauge my reaction.

I put on my most playful face but said nothing.

He continued, "I love it even more because you made it. Made it for me."

He paused and I was speechless.

"So… does this mean you'll finally start teaching me how to use it?" My smile widened at his question. As eager as I was to teach him I was pleased to see how excited he was to learn.

"Yes, I think you're ready to begin using the sword." I took a step closer. "But before we begin, I think we need a little change in our schedule. Just for today at least."

"Please tell me we can skip the running. It's the middle of February and not exactly ideal."

"Well…" I pretend to ponder his request. "Just for today we'll forgo the running. How do you feel about horseback riding?"

He laughed. "Once again you have me at a disadvantage. I haven't been on a horse since I was a kid."

I slinked a step and then another step closer. My voice was huskier than I meant. "I suppose I am used to having you at a disadvantage."

He winked at me playfully. "I have no complaints."

I grabbed his sword and slid it into his sheath. "We're taking swords. Little bit of fun, little bit of work."

Neil helped me saddle two horses. I took the big black gelding that I'd been riding the past month and had taken to calling Halo. Neil took a sorrel gelding named Buck that was actually the gentlest of the small herd.

We rode in silence through the snow for several miles. Flakes fell lightly from the sky and the thick forest of trees opened up to a field.

He looked comfortable in the saddle. Even confident. "I see why you enjoy riding so much."

"Something about being in nature is calming. Riding through the countryside. I suppose it reminds me of home." I was surprised at how at ease I was with him.

Nestled up against the edge of the next stretch of forest was an abandoned barn and cabin I had found on one of my rides.

"There's a wood burning stove in the cabin. I'll start a fire and once we're warm we can begin training in the barn. It's completely empty."

I dismounted from Halo and took the reins from Neil as he dismounted. "I'm from South Dakota. If there's anything I know it's how to start a fire. Why don't you let me do that and I'll let you do whatever it is that you do with horses."

"Fair enough." I walked the horses over to the old trough where a hand pump to a deep well still worked. Once the horses had their fill of water, I took them to the small corral attached to the barn.

I walked into the cabin and instantly warmed. Neil sat in front of the now piping hot stove.

"I found a blanket. Come sit down and get warm." He had removed his coat and only wore his leathers. His chest and arms rippled with muscles that I was constantly aware of. I'd already conceded to giving in to what I felt. So I knelt down.

He reached up and removed my coat. He brought his face to mine. I felt the heat radiate from his skin. His eyes went from mine to my mouth. My breath hitched and at that moment he kissed me. My hands slid his leathers off as he removed mine. Not a spot on either one of our bodies went unexplored. There was a ravenous hunger that had been building for months.

Time was suspended and when we finally lay still Neil rolled me to my back, stroking the hair away from my face. "I love you, Morrigan. I've loved you from the moment I saw you. I was drawn to you the instant I saw the Earth open up and you walked out. As long as I live I am yours. My heart is yours."

I've been in love before. A very, very long time ago. My body was starved for attention and Neil fulfilled my desires. My heart had been closed off for so long. Until this instant I hadn't realized how much so.

"I love you too, Neil." And I kissed him once again.

CHAPTER 8

WE DIDN'T GET to begin our sword training but neither of us had any regrets. We spent the rest of the day and night in the cabin and I was glad I brought more food than we actually needed. It was long overdue for both of us. Emrys was going to be disappointed and King Conall would be livid. By the Creator, I deserved to be happy, even if it was just for a little while. Neil is human and will age while I will not. But hell, we could all be dead in a year's time. I thought I had a happily ever after before and it turned out I was wrong. I will take the little pieces of happiness that I can get when they come along. That's what I've learned after living this long.

The next day, as promised, we began with a run. The energy between us was magnetic and we laughed and talked the entire ten miles. Just like when we began hand-to-hand training, I started with simple defensive blocks with the long sword. Neil was a very quick study and so we began sword strategy and attacks.

We fell into a perfect rhythm. I would slash and he would block, followed by him striking at me while I deflected. His footwork was impeccable. He held the sword I forged for him with strength and grace. Not stiff and rigid like most men did when starting out.

"Very impressive." I still made sure to build his confidence.

This man was a king and was beginning to believe it. I now needed him to be absolute in knowing that he could defeat a God.

"Well I've been fortunate enough to have a very good teacher." He winked and even though I saw it coming I let him sweep my legs, landing me on my back. He grinned triumphantly.

We began most days like this one. A long run followed with training in the stable in the morning. After lunch we began training with the others where he quickly earned their respect and adoration. I spent a few hours with Emrys and King Conall discussing the day then a bit of time with the King's children, catching up. When I returned to my room Neil would be there and we would make love and watch television. I had loads to catch up on and he enjoyed showing his world to me.

The days turned into weeks and weeks into months. Winter had turned into spring and with it the hope that only new life brings. A day came when I woke early, before Neil. Our legs were intertwined and his arm was over me. The cool breeze coming through the window and the sweet smell of morning dew and flowers pulled me out of bed. I got dressed and headed out for a walk by myself.

I realized this was the first time I'd been alone in quite some time. I was either with friends or Neil at all times. I was blissfully happy, but the realization I'd allowed myself to get wrapped up and lost in someone did annoy me. Though I loved to be with others I cherished my time alone and I had forgotten that.

The sun was beginning to crest the hill when from behind a tree stepped Emrys.

"Looking lovely as ever this morning." He nodded at me.

"Did you wake me and lure me here?" I eyed him suspiciously.

"Can't I just have accidentally run into you on such a glorious day?" He evaded my eyes.

I knew at that moment he had. "Jerk." Though I couldn't help but laugh.

He grabbed my hand and we continued on our morning stroll.

"So is this an intervention? Are you worried about me?" I braced myself for his response. I loved Emrys and knew he always had my best interest at heart, which is why I hated when he told me something I didn't want to hear.

His hearty laugh caused his massive chest to bounce up and down. "No, no, no, nothing like that, love. I just wanted some time with you."

I knew Emrys better than that, and I knew he had an agenda.

"How much about you have you shared with him?"

And there it was. Didn't have to wait long. Had anyone else approached me I would have struck them down, but my dearest friend I managed to answer without trying to take his head. "We have enough to do and talk about other than my past, Druid history or anything about the Tuatha. I tell you the truth. Now report it back to King Conall and let's be done with this nonsense."

"Of course, Morrigan. I meant no offense." He smiled, melting me.

I leaned my head against him, soaking his essence up as much as possible. The grass had greened and the fruit trees were all in bloom. Birds sang in a symphony that energized the soul.

"I've not spoken to the King yet, but I will when we meet this evening. I wanted to talk with you first so that you can ponder this and possibly add some insight." I tuned out the song of the birds and perked up, completely focused.

He continued, "I've traveled each night through the Great Oak to most of the large cities around the world. I spent most of my time before you arrived searching for how to awaken the Tuatha and didn't pay much attention to anything else."

He paused and my mind reeled at where this was going. "I've made a couple of observations. How is it that there has been no Tuatha for over a thousand years and yet I've not found many demons? Make no mistake, I've found plenty but not nearly as many as one would think. What I have found, however, is a ton of vampires and werewolves."

The lack of demons was disturbing. It made no sense and I felt we were lacking a lot of information. I'd been so engrossed in training Neil, and let's face it, my love life, that I'd let the big picture slip away. While that nagged at me, I was surprised most about the vampires and werewolves. I'd been watching the movies pop culture was so enamored with and was surprised to find they were real, though I kept my face blank and said nothing.

Emrys, seeing I was not responding elaborated. "Vampires and werewolves have been engineered, Morrigan. They are a cross of several kinds of demons and somehow, someone, or something, has managed to fuse them with humans. Best I can figure it began about five hundred years after we went to sleep."

I finally interjected, "Wouldn't, statistically speaking, this have spread to all the humans in this amount of time?"

He nodded and I could tell he had already considered this. "I thought the same thing. I've caught and questioned a few in the last couple of months."

"So that's what you do all day," I interrupted.

He laughed but otherwise ignored that. "They're highly organized and are not capable of creating new vampires or werewolves on their own. They answer to a king. None I have met know who the king is. They are pretty compartmentalized."

The thought of battling creatures I'd never met filled me with adrenaline. "I think we need to start doing a little recon, then."

CHAPTER 9

I WENT BACK to the room and Neil was sitting up in bed.

"Come here." He extended his hands towards me.

I fastened my long sword down the center of my back with my two medium swords crossing over it. I preferred the medium ones and with two swords, there was nothing that was a match for me.

I leaned down and kissed Neil, but pulled away. "I'm sorry my love, I can't. Change of plans for today. You'll be training with Brian and the group of Knights he's been working with. It's time you begin to learn to fight as a team. To lead them."

I tried to make it sound like it was my plan all along but wasn't sure he bought it. It was a good reason as any, though, and it would be useful for him to begin training with others and not just me.

"What are you going to be doing? I've never seen you use those smaller swords. Why do you have them on?" He was up and getting dressed, the muscles of his body slightly distracting my thoughts.

"I've got some recon to do. I'm not sure when I'll be back. Probably gone a few days. A week at most." I continued placing various knives into my boots.

"Morrigan." He turned me so I faced him. "You're arming

yourself like you're going into World War III. What's going on? And don't say recon. Something's up."

I was going to speak with King Conall and gather a few of my fellow Teulu. Once I had the king's approval, Emrys could take us to these creatures and we could find out what was going on. I loved Neil and I trusted him. But I needed him to focus on his task, which was to learn as much as he could. Not worrying about me.

"Neil, it's all precautionary. I'm more than capable of handling a situation if it should arise. I'll tell you everything when I get back. I love you." And with that I kissed him and walked out, heading to the King's quarters.

It was still early but I knew the King would be awake. I didn't hesitate when I knocked at the door. And kept knocking. And didn't stop until the door flung open with a mostly naked King standing in the doorway looking perturbed.

"Good morning," I said cheerily.

The King stood in his underwear, tall and solid. Anger left his face at seeing me. His eyes lifted and the half grin he reserved for just me when I intrigued him replaced his grimace.

"Morrigan. You seem rather chipper this morning. Why, if I didn't know better I'd say you were excited about something." His grin widened.

I was giddy. Actually bouncing as I stood. I heard Deidra in the background sigh in annoyance as the King mentioned my name. I may have bounced a little higher after that.

I relayed what Emrys had told me, and my plan. I was anxious to see what these creatures were capable of, and to be honest, it had been a long time since I'd come across anything I'd never seen before. That, and as much as I enjoyed training and my time with Neil, I was created for battle. Real battle. I enjoyed hunting, tracking and fighting my enemy. Ridding this world of those that would do harm to others. I thrived on it.

"Can you at least come in so I'm not standing in the hall in my underwear? It's really not regal at all." He opened the door wider.

I entered but couldn't sit. I was too excited. The King never bothered to put on more clothes and the view was not one I minded. I felt the stupid grin on my face, but no matter how hard I tried I couldn't suppress it. Deidra was banging around in the restroom and finally I heard the water run. I found joy knowing I had probably ruined her day. Yay Morrigan!

"So all it takes to make you a happy woman is to agree to let you take five of your Teulu and Emrys on a scavenger hunt for vampires and werewolves?" He was mocking me but I didn't care.

"Yes! Yes that's all that I want. One week's time, maximum. I know this is all tied to us, somehow. I just need to get more pieces of this puzzle." I hated sounding like I was pleading but the King could decide to not let me go and then… oh hell, let's get real, I was going anyway. I knew it and he knew it. But him giving permission would make things much easier.

"You know I trust you, Morrigan." I melted a little every time he used my name and he knew it. Why had I ever told him that? He paused, I know, to let my name linger for a moment before he continued. "I trust you more than anyone on this realm or any other. If this is what you wish then so be it."

I jumped over to him and gave him a hug. He kissed my cheek and pulled away with a serious expression. "We don't know these creatures. I want you to promise me you'll be safe. You'll be methodical and observe before you jump in. You will return unharmed."

"I promise I will return unharmed, as will my men," I vowed. We took promises very seriously. Even the smallest of things were not taken for granted.

"I want *you* to come back unharmed. Promise me, Morrigan, that if you have to, you will save yourself. Even if that means at the cost of another's life." He was serious.

"Conall," I only called him by name without his title when it was just us. "You know I cannot make that promise. I will always fight like hell to stay alive and I fight like hell to keep my people safe. But I could never sacrifice one of them to save myself."

I hoped he wouldn't change his mind. He rubbed his chin with his long fingers. Two days of unshaven scruff. That was my favorite look on him.

He smiled reservedly and nodded. "I guess that's the best I'm going to get from you."

"I'll return in a week or less. Two tops." I started out the door.

I heard him yell down the hall, "Seven days, Morrigan. That's all you get."

CHAPTER 10

WE EXITED THE Great Oak, Daur, my trusted friend at my side. I don't remember his birth name. He had gone by Daur, meaning oak, for as long as I can remember. He was half crazy, strongest of all the Tuatha and as large as a tree. Though many thought him as dumb as a tree, I knew better. He'd been at my back many times. Other than Emrys, he was my closest friend and one of the bravest warriors I knew.

We were in a small park in the French Quarter.

"So this is New Orleans?" I couldn't help the wonder in my voice. I had been watching television, but this was the first modern city I'd actually seen.

"This is it." Emrys beamed. "This is an old part of town. Much magic exists here. I think it's why supernaturals are drawn to it. The humans that have lived here for generations have seen or felt the presence of other realms. It's an anomaly, really. Most humans chalk anything supernatural up to folklore now. But the residents here have their eyes wide open."

The sun was at its highest point in the sky. The weather here warmer than Missouri and I could feel the humidity in the air. The street bustled with jovial energy that somehow simultaneously held a leisurely pace. It definitely was magic.

We strolled down the street wearing modern clothing, our weapons and leathers in large duffel bags. Though we could mirage ourselves against the humans, supernaturals could see past the mirage and we were not about to tip our hand.

"Remember, we're here only to observe and learn what we can." Emrys spoke to us but I knew he was directing the orders to me. I nodded, acknowledging I had heard him. "We'll get a room at a small hotel that is directly across from the vampire and werewolf nest I've found. It's a very large one."

Three days we spent painstakingly noting every member, every pattern, every task they performed. Their nest was more of a small fortress. It was a large hotel that housed a speakeasy style bar at the back of an open garden courtyard. We had taken turns, a couple of us each night, going into the bar for drinks. There was always a small band, lots of dancing and cheap booze. The humans flocked to it.

We sat in our room, Daur stretched out on the bed watching some stupid reality television show. The rest of us were scattered across the floor eating the most wonderful thing I'd ever tasted. Beignets. We could stay here a century stuffing ourselves, and I'd never tire of them.

Emrys clicked away on the laptop at the desk, oblivious to our gluttony. "It seems we have identified seventy-seven vampires and forty-two werewolves. The bar is always packed with humans and around twenty or so supernaturals. Mostly vampire, but five to seven werewolves. Contrary to the lore I've read they are not two separate rival societies. They are one homogenous society that has a symbiotic relationship."

"You sound like a fraking scientist," Daur managed to say with a mouthful of pastry.

Emrys rolled his eyes. "Well, someone around here has to be the smart one. Seeing as you have the big dumb oaf role filled I shall acquiesce to being the intelligent one."

Daur's face was stone. His mouth was caked in powdered sugar, half of a pastry stuck to his beard. His red hair sprayed out as a tangled crown. His eyes radiated rage. The room sparked with tension.

Daur broke the silence by spitting out the rest of his pastry, laughing hysterically with his famous 'mad' look on his face, and I couldn't help but understand why folks thought him nuts. "Druid, you are one funny little man."

Only next to Daur could Emrys be considered little.

"As I was saying," Emrys still looked confused whether the situation was resolved or not, "the myth that vampires cannot be in sunlight holds true. The werewolves stay in all day guarding them. Only two or three will leave throughout the daytime. When the bar opens in the evening it is never the same wolves and vampires that are there. We haven't seen any humans taken from the bar to be fed upon."

"Do the wolves eat the hearts of humans? I saw that in a movie," Daur said with his nose crinkled.

"I don't know any more than you do of their feeding habits." Emrys was now rubbing his temples. I loved Daur and found him amusing. He always got on Emrys' nerves.

"It's been three days and all we know is how many of them there are and where they are," I said, irritated.

"Not exactly," Emrys said a little more smugly than I'm sure he intended. "We can detect what they are by smell. We have sat in that bar, granted, different groupings of us each time, but seemingly have gone unnoticed by them."

Everyone in the room nodded.

"We need more information." My gaze hardened on Emrys. I knew he could spend years sitting in this room observing this nest. I suppose it was being a Druid. Knowledge was a drug to him and acquiring as much of it as he could was his sole purpose at times, it seemed.

"Patience, Morrigan." I felt the magic in his voice and used what defenses I had to not succumb to it. Though he was extremely powerful, I wasn't helpless against these kinds of attacks.

He felt me push back, then gave me his pleading look. The look he gave me when he felt I was being irrational.

Aiden stood up and sat on the foot of the bed. Seeing him next to Daur I couldn't help but notice the contrast. Complete opposites. Aiden followed every order without hesitation, was keenly observant, and fought with textbook precision. Daur's gruffness only made Aiden look 'prettier' and more delicate than he actually was. Daur bathed infrequently and his flaming red hair had never been well kept. Aiden wouldn't dream of leaving his dwelling without looking manicured. He was a trusted Teulu, but I'd take Daur over him any day.

Aiden nodded at Emrys, showing his alignment. "We are, as per the King's request, here to take in as much information as we can. That's all."

I held my impassive mask in place but inwardly rolled my eyes. Daur didn't manage to hold his and stuck his large finger into his nostril behind Aiden, making me laugh.

"Of course." I averted my eyes so as not to give Daur away. "We're only performing recon. Daur and I will take our turn tonight in the bar. He can be my crazy brother in town for a visit from the insane asylum."

Daur always laughed too loud and his eyes bugged out too far when he did so. This time was no exception.

CHAPTER 11

I SLID ON the black high-heeled boots over the equally black jeans I'd brought. Surprisingly, I didn't mind the heels. They took a bit of getting used to but I imagine that in a fight they could take out an eye or stab well if need be. I wouldn't want to run far in them, but they could be a weapon if I had nothing else.

Not having paid much attention to the current fashion I pulled a black t-shirt over my head. Surely all black was acceptable. Now I only had to work on my hair and face. I stared at myself in the mirror for ten minutes. Another ten went by.

"Emrys!" I shouted.

He opened the bathroom door, startled, his hands readied as he looked around for the danger. Not seeing any, his looked puzzled. "What's wrong?"

"I don't know how to put on makeup and I want to try." I had the counter scattered with everything I had bought the day before.

"By the Creator, Morrigan. You scared me half to death. Ask Aiden. He's the pretty one in the bunch. But I warn you, he makes a prettier girl than you."

"You know I can hear you," Aiden growled.

Emrys just winked at me. Any tension from earlier was gone.

"My dear, I have no idea how to put on makeup. But here." He snapped his fingers.

Looking into the mirror I gasped. I looked like a damn drag

queen. He laughed and laughed some more. Then he cried from laughing. I stood staring at him with one side of my mouth raised in a smirk as my eyes cut into him. Most men bent at that look. He laughed harder.

"You can't scare me, looking like that." He gasped for air.

"Okay you've had your fun. Take it off." I still hadn't found amusement in any of this.

With a snap of his fingers I was back to normal. And that was how I would stay.

"Want some help with your hair?"

"No, I'll wear it down. I fear if I ask for your help you'll have it shaped into a swan on my head," I said as I walked out of the bathroom to Daur.

"Daur, you can't go looking like that. You'll make the vampires and werewolves think an ogre has come into their bar and blow our cover," Aiden said, in all seriousness.

Daur had on blue jeans and the biggest canary yellow t-shirt man has ever made that said, 'I Need A Nap.' His hair was disheveled as always and I didn't recall him having bathed since we arrived in New Orleans. That was the Daur I knew.

"Oh, I think you look rather dashing," I gushed as I pulled at his beard and we headed out the door.

We crossed the street, entering the iron gates. As we strode through the courtyard to the bar, and out of the sight of our friends, I flicked my wrist, throwing my hair up into a braided bun.

Daur raised an eyebrow and stopped. Only in movies do people go into battle wearing loose clothing such as capes and long flowing hair. That would surely be a death sentence. An enemy would love to grab your hair with one hand while taking your head with the other.

"I have two knives stashed in each boot. Two for me and two for you." I winked.

His mad eyes widened even more than normal. "Love, you

have four knives for yourself." He lifted his jeans exposing his biker boots. "Got me own knives. I know you were just trying to get me away from the group to have your way with me but I'll have none of that. I came to do a job." He laughed at his own joke. "But I figured when you said *we* were going tonight that you might have a little different definition of 'observing' than them."

His massive hand slapped my back, jarring me forward, spitting as he laughed. I just shook my head. Crazy bugger. I adored him.

The bar was already packed when we entered. Being with a man that towered at seven foot, inconspicuous was not really an option. The good part of that is that when Daur rambled up to a table with four college students and asked if we could join them; they said sure, and promptly got up and left the table to us. Well done, Daur.

"I was friendly was I not?" he asked in all sincerity.

"You were. But even a human can tell you're a predator." I had no underlying meanings in what I said and he tilted his head to the side lifting his eyebrows in understanding.

Quickly shifting the subject he dropped his madness for a serious tone. "You're in love with Neil, aren't you?"

Unlike King Conall or Emrys, Daur was asking me only as a friend. He had no patience for strategy or artifice. No agenda to his question.

"I am," I replied, resigned.

"Good lad." He nodded a firm affirmation of approval. And that was that.

We watched the bartenders—three vampires and two werewolves. Ten servers, all vampires, worked the tables. Three other werewolves were spread throughout the bar, milling about. A vampire sat at the back booth with a werewolf. Three werewolves acted as bodyguards. This was the first time that had happened.

Daur looked like he'd just won the lottery. The music was loud enough that we couldn't hear the vampire or werewolf in the booth. The good news was that they probably couldn't hear us either. At least I hoped their hearing wasn't better than ours.

Daur leaned close to my ear. "You gotta plan?"

"Working on it," I said, with absolutely no plan forming in my head.

The waitress came by to deliver our third round of beers. I thanked her and tipped generously as I had every round and asked in a high-pitched girlish voice, "So are those guys back there like the owners or something?"

The vampire glanced at the booth and back at me. I could tell she was evaluating me. The beat of my heart, the way I smelled, the way I sat. I tried to look as innocent as possible. Daur couldn't help but look like a serial killer. "Something like that." Then she was off.

I glared at Daur knowing he was why I got such a short reply. He smiled, knowing as well, and took a large swig of his beer.

"Well we aren't getting any information this way," I said.

"Bar fight?" Daur said eagerly.

"No!" I squished his hopes. "We need to question someone. But we know who their leaders are now."

I slowly scanned the bar, picking my prey. My eyes stopped on the male vampire bartender. "Him."

CHAPTER 12

WE NURSED A couple more beers. The vampire and werewolf in the booth, along with the bodyguards, left. Last call was announced. I saw the bartender empty the trash, step out from behind the bar and go down the back hall. We followed. There were a few people waiting in line for the restrooms so the bartender had to push through the crowd to go out the back door. The door was on its way to closing as we slid through silently.

The alley was empty. We were behind the building that housed the nest. The old building behind it was another hotel. Apparently they shared this alley and the dumpsters. The bartender turned and jumped, startled, not having heard us.

"Can I help you folks?" he asked in a friendly manner, but I could tell he was on alert.

"Yes, actually." I didn't close the distance, unsure of his skill or strength.

He walked sideways casually, as if he were stalking prey. A smile pulled at my lips at him not realizing he was the one in trouble. But I played my part. I was eager to see what he was capable of.

"I have loads and loads of questions I need answered and I think you're just the gentleman to give me those answers." He paced back the other direction, reminding me of a caged animal evaluating how to strike. He felt superior in his abilities but could tell he was engaging with another predator.

He kept his tone casual. "Well I'm just a bartender but I know the area somewhat. If you're looking for the best jazz in town you only need to go two blocks down. Tell the guy at the door Brandon sent you. He'll hook you up. They stay open until dawn."

"Hmmmm…" I kept my eyes trained on him. "Sounds lovely. But I'm afraid taking in the wonders of your city isn't why I'm here. I need to find out as much information as I can about vampires and werewolves."

He didn't act surprised but grinned, his sharp canines elongating quickly. "I'm afraid you won't live long enough to get many answers."

The vampire was fast. Ten times faster than a human at least. He ran at me and in the blink of an eye was almost upon me. I didn't move. The instant he lunged for me Daur snatched him by his throat and held him two feet off the ground.

"Arsehats have speed." Daur said as the vampire thrashed, his hands pulling at the vice grip Daur's massive hand had on him. "Strong, too. I'm having to work at holding him."

The vampire's eyes were wide. He tried speaking but couldn't get words out.

"Loosen your grip. He's trying to talk and I can't understand a damn thing," I ordered.

Daur loosened only slightly. The vampire's voice was gravelly. "What are you?"

"I'm afraid I said that *I* had the questions. You only get to answer them." I studied him as I spoke. His face was contorted in fear. Fear that he was no longer top of the food chain.

"You don't look like a demon," he croaked out.

We laughed and then heard the back door begin to open. Immediately we looked at one another and jumped to the roof of the neighboring building.

The look on the vampire's face was utter shock. We now stood on the roof, four stories up. Daur tightened his grip so Brandon couldn't make a sound. I feared he would snap the vampire's neck before we questioned him. I peered over the edge. One of the female vampires stepped into the alley, looked around, mumbled, "Lazy asshole," then went back inside.

"Daur, take him to Emrys and have him questioned. I'll be there in a minute," I ordered then jumped back down into the alley.

Daur is one of my favorites because the man never asks any questions. He thrives on battle and absolute mayhem. Any action, no matter how crazy it seems, he just goes with it, never flinching. He knows that plans go awry and never relies upon them. That's why he's a better warrior than Aiden. Aiden thinks plans should be made down to the smallest details and followed, even when the scenario changes. It's his fault as well as a strength, I suppose.

Emrys was going to be pissed. Emrys could adapt in chaos but chose being methodical. I believed in seizing an opportunity and if opportunity didn't present itself, creating it.

I opened the back door. The music had stopped. Quietly I entered the ladies restroom and waited. I heard the front doors being closed and locked. I picked up on seven different voices. Four male and three female. I waited a little longer to be sure. No other voices.

Seven. I wanted to see how they fought. Their strengths, their weaknesses. I only had four long knives. As I sat there waiting, I forced myself to quit wishing I'd brought swords too. Nothing I could do about it now. Time to see if I was in over my head or not. And hope that the other vampires and werewolves would not be alerted.

I pulled two knives out and strode out of the restroom down the hall. I heard them talking. Gossiping about 'Lord Bellamy.' I didn't slow. I threw both knives at the two vampires nearest me, aiming for their hearts. I hit both marks. The vampires instantly turned to ash.

I pulled the other two knives from my boots as the others turned toward me. Two female vampires, a male vampire and two male werewolves.

The vampires unleashed their fangs. The werewolves instantly morphed. I had to focus on not being mesmerized by them. I'd expected them to turn into giant wolves. I kicked myself for watching those ridiculous movies. Stupid teenage girl loves a wolf and a vampire. Both good and both beautiful. They were huge and anything but beautiful. I guess I'd expected them to look more wolf-like. At least ten feet tall, standing on their hind legs like a person would. The fur they sprouted was so black it was as if it actually sucked in any light that tried to get near it. Their heads were definitely canine, and their snouts held teeth as long as my knives. Blood red eyes focused on me. Werewolves weren't wolf at all. They were engineered all right. Part human, part hellhound demon. This was a very, very bad idea.

The werewolf closest to me eyed me as did the other one, but neither moved. It was the vampires who struck first. The female bartender that I'd seen earlier in the alley came directly at me, relying on her speed. I was faster. I stepped to the side and beheaded her as my waitress sped at me. Like her friend, she relied on speed and I easily took her head. The werewolves paced. They might not be wolf, but like all canines, they were pack animals. They would come at me together. The male vampire leaped to the bar and grabbed a lead pipe. Seriously, who keeps a lead pipe lying around? He had learned from his friends. He stood fifteen feet away from me, the wolves at his back. I was betting that the wolves wouldn't attack unless he failed. I was betting my life on it. If I was wrong I would surely die here.

He was faster than the females. My eyes had to focus to keep track of him as he moved. He zigzagged towards me and once in reach, swung the pipe at my head. I ducked and swept his feet.

He fell on his back. I could have taken his head there but I was curious to see him fight, and the werewolves seemed to still only be observing.

The vampire was up in a single blink. This time he didn't swing the pipe but punched for my gut. I fought my training to block the punch, wanting to see how much strength he had. He had a lot. I flew twenty feet, hitting the wall and sliding to the ground. Deciding I had gathered enough information about his strength, and not wanting to go through that again, I lay waiting for his final attack. He was standing above me, both hands on the pipe, ready to plow it down on my head. Thankfully, I moved faster, jumping up and slicing across his neck. The knife wasn't long and not having the force of a full swing, his head teetered halfway off. I raised my other knife, finishing the job so his body could crumble into ash.

I turned towards the wolves. Their hackles were raised and their red eyes bored into mine. I felt a tingle of dread looking into them. One lifted his head and howled. The entire nest would descend in a moment.

"Balls!" I screamed, sprinting towards the back door.

I flung the door open and bumped right into Daur. I felt as if I'd run into a Great Oak and bounced onto my ass. The door behind me flew shut and I heard the werewolves as they crashed into it but it held. Emrys stood with his hands on the door, his face clearly irritated.

"I think it's time for plan B," I gasped, trying to catch my breath.

Emrys, calm as usual only replied, "Clearly."

CHAPTER 13

WE EXITED THE Great Oak in Missouri and had the five mile walk back to the estate. Dawn would be here in a few hours. We hadn't spoken much since our hasty departure from New Orleans. Emrys had been able to spell the exits of the building, sealing them shut until the sun rose.

"So were you able to question the vampire?" I tried breaking the silence.

Daur and the others walked about twenty feet behind us, giving the illusion of privacy.

Emrys looked sideways at me. "Why am I always surprised at you? I clearly... no, King Conall clearly stated we should go and observe these creatures. Not go in like a God damned wrecking ball into a fortress you know nothing about with creatures you know even less about. I'm as livid as a fire demon. You could have been killed in there. If your intentions were to go into battle you don't do it alone. You know this."

He was right. I took a deep breath and exhaled through my teeth.

I conceded but kept my tone cool, "You're right, Emrys. It was rash and wrong."

I heard Aiden give a, "Hmph," sound and I turned, throwing a knife next to his boot. Okay, it actually hit his boot but didn't pierce the skin. I did have expert aim, after all.

I was on him before he could react. Still keeping my voice emotionless I warned, "Remember yourself, dear Aiden. Watch well."

Emrys hadn't moved. Hadn't reacted even. He just waited until I walked back to him. I heard nothing from anyone behind us.

Emrys didn't make a sound, but his chest bounced as he chuckled silently. "I can't imagine why you go centuries between men. I mean you're such a warm, inviting, delicate little flower."

I rubbed my shoulder on his as we walked until he put his arm around me. He sighed, forgiving my actions.

"I learned much from the vampire. A lot actually. Your little... plan? No that's definitely not the word. Your massively blundered debacle... yes, yes, that's the more accurate, was rather fruitful. Once we get back we'll meet with the King and I'll go over everything."

This was his little way of torturing me. We had miles to walk and he could tell me everything but would make me wait. I hated waiting, and he knew it.

I was tired and still covered in dried black blood from the vampires I'd killed when we arrived at the front door. Someone had seen us coming, three days earlier than expected, and alerted the others. That's what I'm guessing since Neil raced out the door with a panicked look on his face.

I'm sure I was a sight. I could feel my hair, face and neck crusty with the blood, my clothes still damp from it. The vampires, like demons, had the thick black muck coursing through their veins. I'd never understood how they could gush so much of it out as you sliced their heads off and their bodies turned to ash—you were left covered in the filth. Emrys had given me an explanation once but after a few minutes I got bored and quit listening. He was always so intrigued with how things worked.

Neil stopped short of me, cupping my face in his hands. "Are you okay? Are you hurt? What happened?"

I smiled and assured him, "I'm fine. It's not my blood."

I grabbed his hands and lowered them. He was shaking. His look melted me. His concern for my well being warmed me.

The King and his children, but not Deidra, were on the front steps. The children smiled at me and I smiled back with a wink.

The King had his half smirk on his face. That look. It melted me in its own way as well. This could go either way. He could be mad as hell or being playful. After centuries I'd still never quite figured out the subtle difference. I would soon find out as he spoke. "So I see the observing went well. Tell me, did you stealthily watch and learn much without them knowing you were there?"

I stood unmoving. I kept my face devoid of emotion until I could figure out where this was going.

He walked slowly towards me. Neil had come to stand at my side. My King stopped in front of me and raised his hand to my hair. "You look much better as a redhead, but if you wanted to become a brunette all you needed to do was ask Emrys. I'm sure he could've managed a spell, rather covering yourself in demon blood."

Aine giggled at her father's joke which made the King lose his control and start laughing as well. The half smirk was playful... this time. Thank the Creator.

The few that had gathered on the front lawn laughed. Except Neil. Neil was not amused. Not at all. His face held concern and rage all at once.

"Go get cleaned up, then eat. We'll meet in three hours in the library. All of you." He looked at our little group, nodding.

Neil grabbed my hand and we walked in silence to my room. Entering it, I could tell he had been staying there the four days I was gone. The thought made me smile.

He shut the door then hugged me tight. The embrace held no heat, no desire, just comfort and caring. Love. Then he held me at arm's length, anger in his eyes. "Morrigan? You're covered in...

in… demon blood? You were supposed to go and study vampires and werewolves."

He stared, waiting for an answer.

"It's vampire blood. They're part demon so their blood is black as well," I answered.

"That's all you have to say? Correcting me, 'Oh no Neil, not to worry, it's not demon blood, it's only vampire blood.' Really? That makes it all right? Never mind, I shouldn't be scared out of my mind after all." He screamed the last few words.

I loved that he cared about me. I loved that he was worried about me. I let him yell for another half an hour or so, not saying a word. I knew he had to release his feelings. That bottling them up would only cause a distance between us. So I sat in silence as he bounced between lashing out at me and pouring his heart out to me. When he was done he sat down on the edge of the bed.

I kneeled at his feet and looked up at him. "I love you," is all I could manage to say.

I got up and went the bathroom. The damn vampire blood was just as sticky as demon blood and not easy to wash out. Even with modern soap and shampoo it took forever. Finally, I got out of the shower and once back in the room, I saw Neil had left. I was ready to head out to eat when Neil came back in.

"Hey, I didn't know where you went." Now clean, I wrapped my arms around his neck and lifted my face up to kiss him.

He gave me a quick peck and slowly took my arms off of his neck, walking to the other side of the room. "I have training to get to. I'll see you tonight."

He grabbed his weapons and left. Not wanting to share the walk with him I sat down on the bed. I was so tired. I was drained. Physically and emotionally. I was not good in these situations and unsure how best to handle them.

I went to the Cauldron and grabbed a roasted turkey leg. It dripped fat as I bit into it. It was heavenly. I glanced at my watch and realized I hadn't time to sit so I ate as I walked towards the library.

Daur met me in the hall. "Is that turkey? Give me a bite," he said as he grabbed it from me. His eyes closed as he sunk his teeth into it. He smiled as the fat dripped down his chin, soaking his beard.

"God it's a wonder that the ladies don't just flock to you," I teased.

"The ladies love me. Can't get enough of me. It's my good looks and charm. You're fortunate that I haven't used my charms on you," he teased back.

We were the last to enter the library. The merry mood left us as we stepped across the threshold. Everyone having their blank faces on, we put ours on as well. I did at least, Daur tried, but his beard still had the lingering fat and he kept sticking his tongue out trying to get at it.

King Conall did as he always did and stared at Daur, amazed that the man had been able to stay alive as long as he had. He shook his head and spoke to Emrys, "Well, what did you learn, questioning the vampire?"

If Emrys were a human born in modern times he would have been a scientist. He could study anything, getting bogged down in the most minute of details. He thrived on figuring out how things worked. I only cared what was. Not the why or how behind it. I had to remind myself that though we had been friends for centuries and I myself was quite old, he was much, much older. He was around when things were still being created and the magic of it all intrigued him.

Knowing the King was much like myself I breathed a sigh of relief as he began, not going off on tangents, only relaying the necessary facts. "The vampire Morrigan and Daur captured was not very high up in their society. But he was well informed. I was able to use magic and secure his memories. I couldn't do that from a full demon but since he was part human, I was able to. That surprised me."

I could tell Emrys wanted to explore his theories on that but he stopped himself and continued. "Each large city has a Lord that rules over it. Some of the smaller cities have a Lord that presides over a few cities. Since New Orleans has a large vampire and werewolf population, Lord Bellamy rules over it solely. The Lords answer to a King. There is a King for each region, five total: North America, South America, Africa, Europe and part of Asia, and finally one for the Far East and Australia. The Kings answer to a Prime. The vampire did not know who the Prime is. Only the Kings do. And only the Kings are capable of creating other vampires or werewolves. So the lore of being bitten by one and getting turned is false. Pure myth."

"And the process of becoming a vampire?" the King asked, while giving Emrys his 'keep the answer short' look.

Emrys nodded understanding. "This is a little lengthy but I'll try to keep it simple. Funny thing about there being few demons around these days. Apparently they've been locked up in another realm. Hell, as the humans call it, is real. It's just another realm, but it does exist. The Gods trapped as many demons as they could and locked them in this realm. They are physically there. But they are able to visit this world with their… essence? Let's just say their essence. A human has to give their permission. So, they are usually someone that has had a great loss or that is desperate in some manner or another. The demons have been doing this in order to continue to feed themselves and survive. The Gods apparently didn't know they would be able to do this. Why they didn't just end them is beyond me. But you know the Gods. Anyhow, the person the demon possesses is coexisting so it's not a complete takeover. The demon can only influence the person. They begin by offering comfort, advice or fill whatever void the person has. Then they begin the constant unrelenting whispers to get the person to take another human's life. Once the person has taken a life, they convince that individual to kill themselves. Once they have, the demon consumes their soul. That's how they feed themselves."

"Well that's just awful," Aiden said.

Emrys continued, "Once in a while the demon possesses a person with attributes they consider... well honorable isn't the right word. Let's say, worthy. The person is usually attractive, in good health and strong. A specific event has left them desperate so they consent to the possession. For instance, the vampire I questioned was overcome with grief from seeing his fiancé killed in a car accident. He was driving, and although it was a drunk driver that hit them, he still blamed himself. These are the types of situations that the demons are looking for. The person has to completely consent to the possession. When the demon has tried and tried, spending all their efforts for the person to take another's life and that person does not, then they are a candidate to become a vampire or werewolf. They are looking for those that are strong in will. The bizarre thing is, that the memories I took from the vampire knew all of this but had no knowledge or memory of the actual process it took to become one. Like it was blocked out. But a Vampire King was the one that all vampires and werewolves went to in order to be turned."

"This is so bizarre," Daur said, now sitting on the edge of his seat like we were telling campfire stories.

"Seriously twisted stuff." Emrys agreed. "And here's the kicker. They believe themselves to be part of an army in order to save the Earthly realm. To save this realm and the people in it."

"Okay, now that is the craziest thing I've heard in centuries," I couldn't help adding.

Emrys held up his hands as we all started to speak. "They do not see themselves as saviors or heroes. Humans are their food source. The vampires don't kill the humans they feed on. They only take about as much as when a human donates blood. Less actually. They have enough magic in them to erase the memory from the human, replacing it with a pleasant experience. The marks still remain, which is why they are usually not on the neck but on the wrist or the femoral artery."

I could see Daur was clueless so I grabbed his inner thigh. He nodded and winced at the same time.

"And the werewolves?" King Conall asked.

Emrys continued, "The werewolves feed upon the flesh of the demon-possessed humans once they kill themselves. So the vampires, werewolves and demons need the humans. But that doesn't explain why they feel adamantly that they are an army in the cause of saving the entire human race."

"Obviously there is much we don't know." King Conall paced and stroked his chin. "So how did this vampire you questioned get picked to be a vampire and not a werewolf? Did he know?"

Emrys was already answering before the King finished his question. "Apparently that's any easy decision. If the person is an average Joe, say, never having taken a life or committing any horrific act, then they become a vampire. To become a werewolf is much more difficult which is why there seem to be fewer of them. Again, the person possessed must withstand the demon's demands to kill another. The difference is that prior to the possession, the person must have taken a life, or lives, in a manner that was not in wrath or revenge. For instance, a warrior, soldier or assassin would make a likely candidate. They do not kill for personal gain, they're not emotionally invested and probably don't even know who they're killing. That is the kind of person that would become a werewolf. That's why they're more deadly. Soldiers, like the pack animals, work together for the greater good, put more value on their compadres lives than their own, and are fearless."

"And they are *not* wolves," I said, seeing as this was as good a time as any.

"Werewolves. They are werewolves. What part of that word makes you think they're not wolves?" Aiden said in his crisp, pretty little voice.

"Because while you were admiring your reflection back in the hotel, I was in a room with them." I respected Aiden as a warrior and his loyalty to our people. As a person I thought him shallow and arrogant. To say the least, I didn't care for him.

I continued. "I saw two shift into their werewolf form in the bar. They stood about ten feet high and on two legs. Their canine faces, the blood red eyes, the blackness of their fur, their smell. They, like the vampires, are part human. But the other half are definitely hellhound."

There were a few gasps but nobody said anything. Hellhounds were some of the fiercest demons. The fact that they were fused with experienced hardened soldiers probably made them more deadly rather than their human blood diluting their strength.

"How did they fight?" King Conall asked, worry reflected in his eyes.

"I didn't get the chance to engage them." I glanced at Emrys, he was captivated and I knew he would question me relentlessly later about everything I could remember. "When I went back into the bar there were five vampires and the two wolves."

I told them the story as accurately as I remembered. Every detail.

The King absorbed every ounce of information. Unlike Emrys, the King wasn't one to acquire information just to have it. He planned to use it and exploit it. That's why he was King. "So the vampires you experienced were untrained fighters. They rely on their strength and speed, but we are faster and stronger. More skilled and experienced. That's good. The werewolves, though. They could've easily pounced on you while you were in a skirmish with the vampire but did not. They only observed."

The King stopped but we could tell he was not finished with his thought. "Then one howled, I assume to communicate to the others. They didn't move towards you until you ran towards the back door."

"They didn't know what you were. They were curious," Emrys interrupted.

The King added to the thought. "Yes, they were curious, and they wanted to capture you rather than destroy you. Emrys, you said that the vampires and werewolves couldn't smell us. That we smell just like humans to them. I imagine that the wolves had never seen a human move faster than a vampire, nor match its strength."

"So much for the element of surprise," Aiden said, opening the door for the King to chastise me in front of all the Teulu.

The King's blue eyes stabbed into Aiden's. Without even speaking, the King forced the pretty warrior to shrink into his chair. He was on him in an instant and bent over to within an inch of Aiden's face. Barely above a whisper he said, "We have lost no element of surprise. Because of Morrigan's actions we have gained more information than I'd hoped for. What did you find out, Aiden? What piece of knowledge did you bring back?"

Aiden was no fool. He kept silent.

The King stood up straight, still looking at Aiden. "That's enough for now. Everyone go."

We all rose and strode towards the door. The King gently grabbed my arm. "Morrigan, stay a moment, will you?"

I heard the politeness in his voice. I imagine this was for the others' benefit. Not mine.

The last Teulu left, shutting the door behind him.

King Conall walked over to an overstuffed leather chair and plopped onto it. He looked tired. He leaned his head back and closed his eyes. I walked to the chair and sat on the edge of the armrest. He was beautiful and I loved him. I was in love with Neil, but I loved my King. He would always hold a special place in my heart. Keeping his eyes closed, he held his hand out for me to take. I took it and held it in my lap. He slowly drew circles with his thumb on the back of it.

I softened at the gesture. I was afraid to break the silence. To end the moment. But as all moments do, they pass.

King Conall kept his head leaned back but opened his eyes. "Morrigan, Morrigan, Morrigan. Woman, you will be the death of me yet."

"Don't say that. Not even in jest, Conall," I said in all seriousness.

He did his little half smile. The playful one I was sure of. "I am serious. We needed the information that you were able to gather. But by The Creator, did you really need to be so rash? I warned you. Hell, I ordered you to be careful. You and I know damn well that was careless."

I opened my mouth but he beat me. "If Aine were to have done as you did? Or either of the boys? Would you let them?"

I stayed sitting on the arm of the chair but I turned, putting my feet onto his lap so I could face him. "No. I would not. I would not let any of them do as I did."

The King's face welcomed my concession but still held concern.

I softened my voice as best I could. "Conall, I wouldn't have let any Tuatha do what I did. Which is why I was the one that did it. There is something, something realm-shattering coming. I feel it. I took a risk that even I was not comfortable with. But I have this feeling deep within me that we are in a giant puzzle that is shifting and moving, and we need to figure it out quickly."

The King kept his hand on mine and his other he rested on my boot. He didn't look regal at the moment. He looked harried. He reminded me of how my father looked at times when he was King. The weight of not only his people, but the entire realm, on his shoulders. I would do anything to help lighten that burden.

Conall nodded. "Morrigan, I feel it too. I'm scared."

There was no use of either of us trying to mask what we were feeling. We worked well together because we were always honest. Even when it was hurtful. But the King had to show strength to his people, to his children, to Deidra. He could just be himself with me. I cherished these moments even when they were in times of distress. I felt that I had a piece of Conall that nobody else did. That nobody else ever could.

"Be scared, Conall," I said, stroking his golden hair. "Be scared tonight. But by the time you leave this room be done with it. By the Creator, we did not survive this many centuries, through hundreds of battles, to go down now. I know you hate taking unnecessary risks, like what I did in New Orleans. Hell it's my ass on the line. I hate taking those kinds of risks. But you have to give me leave to do so. We are at such a disadvantage right now. Not only are there forces we don't know or understand at work, we live in a damn world that we don't even know anymore. I feel like I'm in a bad dream. Sent to a far off realm, and I just want to make my way back home. There is no more home, though. It's over a thousand years away. It's not a place we can ever go to or visit other than in our memories."

"You're right, Morrigan." He smiled up at me. "So was that your 'get your head out of your ass' and 'let me do what I damn well want' speech all rolled into one?"

I couldn't help but let out a long overdue laugh.

"I miss that laugh. Your laugh comes from deep within." He patted my boot.

"Well if you weren't King you could go out on missions with us like you used to." I winked.

The King's fiery eyes met mine and I knew if I gave the slightest indication that I'd let him kiss me he would. I loved him, but that kind of love was not mine to have. Not now.

I tried to think of something to pull his attention away from his current thoughts but for the second time tonight he spoke first. "Do you remember when we were tracking that incubus demon across Scandinavia? We got caught in that blizzard but managed to make it to that little village."

I knew where this conversation was going. I saw the lust in his eyes and could feel the bulge under my foot growing.

"We were both just soldiers, early in our years. Wild in our ways. You were a fierce warrior and now you are a great King." I slowly and nonchalantly swiveled off the chair and stood. "I'm going to go get some rest, my King."

I felt like the mouse must when the cat has batted at it and let it slip away… momentarily.

Chapter 14

IT WAS EARLY afternoon and the sun shone brightly. Spring, the smell of life, held strong in the air. I closed the door to my room. Neil was still in training. I hoped he would return here, rather than his room, once he finished. The breeze caught the curtains as they danced along the wall and I fell into the down bedding.

I woke startled. The room was pitch black. I looked at the clock—the red numbers glared back at me: 11:22 pm. I stayed still, my ears and eyes alert. What had woken me? Once I'd deemed the room safe and myself alone I turned the lamp on. I still missed candlelight. I still missed what I used to call home. Or rather the time that I had called home.

I knew Neil wasn't here before I scanned the room. I felt silly doing it anyway. I was only gone a few days but the distance I felt from Neil felt like a canyon. My heart ached to touch him. To just be near him. This was not the homecoming I'd expected.

I was still in my clothes from earlier. I got up and undressed myself. I was so immersed in my pity party I paid no attention to the steps coming down the hall or the doorknob turning.

"Well hello there, beautiful," Neil said, dropping his gear and quickly scooping me up.

I wrapped my legs around his waist and kissed him.

He finally pulled back a little and sat down on the bed. I kept my legs around his waist. I couldn't let him go.

He pushed a stray strand of hair away from my face. "I've never seen you sleep so hard. I came back after dinner and was afraid I'd wake you. I found Brian and he agreed to help me with some additional... Well I'm not going to tell you." His grin reached his eyes. "I've learned a few things. I'll just have to keep those up my sleeve for the next time we spar."

He grabbed hold of my butt to lift himself up enough to roll me on my back and kept me pinned securely under him.

He kissed me lightly and leaned his forehead to mine, closing his eyes. "I wish you could stay right here in my arms for always. I'd never have to worry about you. I love you with my entire heart. It's yours, Morrigan. I cannot imagine living in this world without you in it. I'm sorry about earlier. I didn't mean to seem like I was yelling at you. I... I wasn't mad at you. I was scared. Terrified at the reality that I could lose you. I know you can fight. You're my mentor, for crying out loud. I'm not an idiot. I just want you safe and with me."

We didn't say another word that night. Nor did we sleep much.

We were slow to wake the next morning and I finally dragged myself from the bed to the shower. My heart swelled. That's the only way I can describe it. I only realized I was still smiling when my cheeks began to tire. I didn't care that I was acting like a schoolgirl. I was happy. It had been a very long time since I was happy in this manner.

The door opened and Neil got in the shower. "So what's the plan, boss? Wanna go for a horseback ride and find that little cabin at the edge of the forest?" He kissed me again. I couldn't help but laugh.

"As much as I'd rather do that, I'm afraid not." I kissed him again just because he was near me. "I have some planning to do with Emrys. You'll continue to work with Brian and your men. You need to learn to work as a unit, so you must train as one."

"I'd still much rather train with you." He began washing my back. I'd already washed it. I didn't care. I let him.

Still caught up in the high I felt this morning I tried to continue. "You are all learning and will continue to learn fighting but you must learn the strength of working together. Did you know the Spartans didn't care if a soldier lost a helmet or weapon on the battlefield, but if he lost his shield he would be killed upon returning? The helmet and weapons were to protect the soldier. The shield, though useful in battle, was one of their greatest strengths. It was a single piece in building a shield wall. To protect the entire unit. They valued the group over the individual. Pay close attention to Brian. I don't only mean just what he's teaching you. Study how he acts, how he commands. You are the King of Erin, Neil. Never forget that."

Somehow escaping without having sex one more time, I went straight to Emrys' room. He opened the door, in typical Emrys style, with magic, before I could even knock.

"I swear sometimes you sound like an elephant tromping through the jungle when you walk," he said, not even looking up from the desk.

"I do not. I'm as light as a hippo," I said, walking to his side to see what he was studying.

Notes on vampires and werewolves from our recon mission. From the looks of him he'd been up all night, which explained his foul mood.

"You need coffee and breakfast," I said, trying to snap him out of it.

Once again, without looking away from the papers, he snapped his fingers and a carafe of coffee and a tray of muffins appeared on the desk.

"I'm not amused, asshole." I had no humor in my voice. He finally looked at my face to see my expression. I was smiling and he rolled his eyes.

I could tell he was not in the mood to be toyed with, so I

tried to mirror his energy. "Emrys, put the notes down for a minute and listen to me. I know we need to learn more about the vampires and werewolves. But I also know that you could study them for a hundred years and still not be satisfied you have enough information."

He held his hands up to stop me. He was tired but his face radiated gentility. "I know, Morrigan. I know I can get carried away. I just…"

I cut him off, knowing my news would lighten his mood. "We're going to get all of your questions answered. Okay, well not all of them. You no doubt have thousands. But we're going to figure out what we *need* to know."

He leaned back, crossing his arms over his chest. "I'm intrigued. Go on." He smiled.

"Brian is training Neal along with the Knights. It's time they begin fighting together. Brian can handle that. We need to start focusing on the vampires and werewolves. We have about six months until Samhain. That time is now dedicated to this mission."

He stood and circled me as he talked. I could tell he was eager but hesitant. "And your King? You think he will go along with this?"

He stopped in front of me raising an eyebrow, watching me closely. "I spoke to King Conall last night after we debriefed. He agreed to let me do whatever I needed in order to attain the information."

"He did?" A smile pulled at his lips but he held it back. "Conall hit on you didn't he?"

"Oh for crying out loud, Emrys." I unleashed my eyeroll at him.

"HA! I knew it!" he exclaimed. "He hit on you and when that didn't work he agreed to let you have what you wanted. I swear that man will do anything to get you into bed. Does Neil know—"

Once again I cut him off. I didn't want him to finish his question. "Don't bring Neil into this," I said, too harshly.

"Okay no need to get your blood pressure up." He was done teasing me. "I won't bring it up again."

"I'm sorry. I didn't mean to snap at you." I shook my head.

"No need for apologies, love. You just made me the happiest man in the realm. When do we start?"

"Today." I beamed at making him this happy.

CHAPTER 15

THE NEXT THREE months were busy. We had devised teams of Tuatha to go through the Great Oak into various cities around the world and identify as many vampire and werewolf nests as we could. We'd report back to Emrys and he'd click away on his laptop, detailing every piece of information. When he wasn't doing that, he was busy training the Druid descendants in using their magic beyond healing. They would need to learn to defend themselves in the coming war.

I would go out with my team: Daur, Aiden, Miranda, Jillian, and Donnell for three days at a time on surveillance. Aiden took on the role of reporting back to Emrys. I did like having Aiden on my team for that reason if no other. He'd loosened up a bit and seemed less offended by Daur's 'charms.' The rest of the week I'd spend with Brian, watching over the training of the Knights and Neil. I always looked forward to returning—spending time with Neil was the highlight of my week. He hadn't gone to his room in months and it held nothing of his anymore.

I walked into the training arena after having returned and stood next to Brian. We both had our eyes on the group of six that were about to be attacked in a simulation by twelve Tuatha. I snuck a glance at Brian. He was stoic as ever. I couldn't help but smile as I spoke. "You're advancing them quite rapidly don't you think?"

Brian risked a smile, he didn't do that often so when he did, it especially delighted me. "Just watch."

Neil was in the group of six. They were perfectly synchronized in their defense as the dozen Tuatha attacked. The King's orders of keeping our strengths and skills a secret still held, so the Tuatha fought at a matching level against the Knights.

Brian cleared his throat as we continued watching. "Neil has truly become a leader. Their King. Watch how he will shift from defending to attacking and the others follow."

I nodded, and as Brian predicted, Neil began a beautiful attack. He was strong, stronger than most humans. His execution of each swing of the sword was precise and graceful. His face never contorted in anger or showed any signs of fatigue, but rather intense duty, focusing his energy at the task at hand.

Brian continued, "The rules are, once struck with the wooden sword you are considered fallen and are 'out.'"

Neil continued slicing through the Tuatha. He hit one of the Tuatha on the shoulder as he leapt on top of him, only to jump further towards the onslaught and took out two more swiftly.

I recognized the move as one of Brian's signature attacks. He nodded approvingly. This must be what Neil was so excited about having learned.

The Knights and Neil defeated the Tuatha in the mock battle. I raised my eyebrow to Brian. He only shrugged. "Occasionally they must win. It is best to continue to bolster their confidence."

I nodded, this time in agreement.

He said, "The Druids are going to begin training with us soon as well. Emrys is working on teaching them to slow down vampires so that the humans might actually have a chance at fighting them. He's also working on a few other spells they may be able to handle. They'll need to be incorporated into our fighting, and not just as healers."

"Sounds logical," I agreed, though not completely sure that was the best plan.

"Well done, Knights." Brian shouted in his gruff, gravelly voice. "That's enough for today. You've earned the rest of the day off. Go enjoy yourselves, but be ready tomorrow morning."

The Knights were jubilant at having won. The Tuatha were congratulating them and they intermingled, verbally replaying every move. It warmed me to see them together.

Neil saw me and approached. He looked amazing. Sweat lightly glossed his tanned body. His muscles got larger and more defined every time I returned, it seemed. His caramel eyes sparkled with the remaining excitement of battle. He was now in his element. I couldn't help but think of how different this man, this King, was from the one I met not that long ago.

"How's the love of my life?" he said, grabbing my waist, lifting me up to kiss him.

"Very fortunate to not have been fighting vampires as skilled as you and your men." I couldn't help tease.

He laughed, shaking his head. "We aren't quite at that level yet, but we will be." He was completely confident. No doubt or arrogance in his voice. It was said only as a fact.

He continued, "Well it would seem I have the rest of the day off." His eyes never left mine and the twinkle from battle turned into a flame that only I knew.

"Whatever will we do with ourselves?" I asked with a slow smile.

"It's summer, and we haven't gone swimming in the lake yet. How about we have a picnic and head there?" he asked with eagerness in his eyes.

Memories washed over me from so many years ago of leisurely spending time near a lake. Enjoying the warmth that came with summer. It sounded perfect.

The day went too fast. We were able to be alone at the lake for about an hour when everyone else had the same idea. That was fine. My belly and face hurt from laughing at hearing the stories of how their training was going. Once the sun began to sink low in the sky we built a bonfire and brought the cauldron out to continue the festive evening. I hadn't gotten to know many of the humans so it was delightful to see them hang on every word Neil spoke. Many of the Tuatha joined in as well. I tried to savor the moment. To hold onto it. Humans, Druids and Tuatha all gathered here, laughing. Daur was surprisingly a huge hit, and one of the Druid girls was practically draping herself over him. I was slightly solemn at knowing this would come to an end. That many would lose their lives in the coming war. I pushed the thought from my head but it kept creeping back.

CHAPTER 16

THE TREES TURNED glorious oranges, reds and deep purples as crispness in the air replaced the lazy humidity of summer. Samhain had arrived.

It was a very important holiday for us. One of great feasts and celebrations. I was saddened that I would miss the festivities, but more anxious about being away for the span of a year. The entire grounds bustled as preparations for the great feast were being made. There would be bonfires, wine and roasted meats. Music, dancing and laughing would rule the night. The Royal family would begin the ceremony by walking through the crowd to light the first bonfire and all would cheer. The humans and Druids had the extra excitement of this being their first Samhain.

The official start would be after sunset. The moment the sun disappeared from the horizon would be when Emrys and I would enter the Great Oak to the realm between twilight and night to seek out Druantia.

It was late afternoon and Emrys, Brian, the King and myself were in the library going over plans.

Emrys cleared his throat before he spoke. "Riley is the best and brightest of the Druids that I have, and will continue to work with the others. Brian, I will trust you to make sure that the Knights and Druids become a single working unit for battle."

Brian nodded and grunted his affirmation.

King Conall leaned back in his chair. "We'll continue the training. Brian will decide progressions of the group over the course of the year. I will personally oversee the recon of the vampires and werewolves. Morrigan, you and Emrys will hopefully come back with the location of my sword. I fear that without the Sword of the Tuatha there is no hope of defeating Artaius. Somehow, Artaius, the vampires and werewolves are connected. By the Creator let's hope Druantia has the answers for us."

We got up to leave as Treasach, Alastar and Aine entered the library.

Alastar grabbed me in a bear hug, lifting me off the ground then setting me back down. "You didn't think you were going to leave for a year without a proper goodbye did you?"

My heart leapt into my throat as my eyes misted. Treasach and Aine joined in the hug. The King stood back on his heels with his hands on his waist, smiling.

Aine pulled her head away from my cheek just enough to look at me in the eyes. "Have you ever been to this realm before?"

"No. I promise to remember every detail and next Samhain when I see you, I'll tell you all about it," I said, then pulled her head back to me.

Treasach towered over us and his bright blue eyes bored into mine as he spoke. "This will not be a true Samhain celebration without you. Next year, we'll wait on your return and will not begin until you arrive. As it should be."

The King walked over, placing his hand upon his son. "Treasach is correct. It is not a true Samhain without you. The Druids and Knights will have no idea what next year's celebration will hold." He placed his other hand upon Emrys and asked, "Can we count on a little help from you to make next year's Samhain extra special?"

Emrys smiled and bowed. "I promise you, King Conall, that it will be one that even the Tuatha will be breathless at."

I said my goodbyes to Treasach, Alastar and Aine. Emrys

walked out of the library with them but I stayed behind to speak to the King alone.

I shut the door and turned. "Conall..." The lump in my throat had grown so large I couldn't manage to speak. Silent tears began to roll down my cheeks.

The King wrapped his arms around me and softly kissed the top of my head, then barely above a whisper said, "Morrigan, I know you hate to miss a year. Especially after our long... our long sleep where we missed centuries. I know you also fear that you will be too late. But this is *my* 'Get your head out of your ass' speech to you." He pulled back to look at me. "I have faith in you. You above any other Tuatha will succeed. And I need you to have faith in me. Have faith that in the time that you are gone I will have gathered more answers. Can you trust in me?"

I didn't hesitate. "My King, I have never wavered in my trust for you. I know that you will."

He smiled down at me. "I mean it. Samhain will feel hollow without you. Though we traditionally start at sunset, we will wait for your return from the Great Oak to begin next year."

He leaned down and kissed me on the cheek. It wasn't quite a chaste kiss but at least it was not on the lips.

My heart was lighter, feeling secure that things would progress in my absence.

"Until next Samhain, my King. Watch well," I said as I exited the room.

I stopped to say my goodbyes to the team that I'd spent the last few months tracking vampires and werewolves with. Daur cried like a baby. Like the King, he promised that next Samhain would be the true celebration. I promised I'd dance with him and he went from crying to his mad laugh. Even Aiden seemed emotional and actually hugged me, though he immediately looked embarrassed. I was warming to him.

The sun kept getting lower in the sky as I made my way to my room. My hardest and last goodbye. Neil.

I entered the room to find him sitting on the edge of the bed. His caramel eyes looked heavy. His light brown hair was a bit longer than when I'd first met him and I longed to run my hands through it.

He held his hand out and whispered, "Come here."

I walked over, taking his hand, and he pulled me onto his lap. He stroked the side of my face, down my neck and rested his hand over my heart. "Morrigan, so much has happened over this past year. It's gone so fast. Too fast. I've known this day was coming and now that it's here—"

"I know." I interjected. "There's something I need to... tell you." The words of Conall and Emrys about keeping my, our, history a secret for now reverberated in my mind. I caught myself. *I'll tell him upon my return*, I vowed. Instead I said, "It's only a year, though. Listen to Brian and continue to lead your Knights and work with the Druids."

"I know what I need to do." He kept his eyes intently focused on mine. He seemed to not notice my near stumble. "I just don't want to do it without you. What will it be like for you?"

I stayed in his lap. His hand made its way to my back, rubbing it lightly. "Well, for me it will only seem like an hour. I've never been to the realm between night and twilight so I'm not really sure what to expect."

"Will you be safe?" he asked.

"Yes, it's safe," I said, now rubbing his chest. "Druantia is there alone. I'm not sure if she's unable or unwilling to leave. Regardless, there are no enemies there."

"That seems so lonely."

"I suppose it is," I said, leaning down to kiss him.

His lips were soft. I could feel the heat building in them as the tenderness dropped away. I leaned him back onto the bed and slowly soaked him in. For me it would seem like only a few hours from now we would be making love again. But I knew for him, a human no less, a year was a long time and I wanted to ease the ache in his heart with enough physical love to sustain him.

We finished making love, then I began to get ready for the five mile trek to the Great Oak. We would be taking horses and needed to be at the stables in twenty minutes.

"Neil, I know it would mean you missing the beginning of your first Samhain celebration but would you ride with me to the Great Oak?" I asked, realizing I sounded like I was pleading. I was, though.

"Morrigan, for you I would ride to the ends of the Earth." he said as he began to dress.

CHAPTER 17

EMRYS, BRIAN, NEIL and myself set out on horseback to the Great Oak. The horses felt the energy of Samhain and made good time.

Emrys and I dismounted and gave the reins of our horses to Brian and Neil.

"We will need to enter in less than a minute," Emrys said, looking at me. I know he felt my uneasiness.

Neil hopped from his horse and gave me one last embrace. As he pulled away he cupped my face and with a seriousness I'd never seen from him said, "One year's time, my love. I will be right here a year from now. I love you."

I know my eyes teared a little. I didn't mind Emrys seeing, but thankfully Brian looked away, clearly uncomfortable. I ran my hand through Neil's hair and said, "One year. I love you."

"Now, Morrigan," Emrys said, grabbing my hand.

Then we entered the Great Oak.

We came out into the realm between night and twilight. You could feel the magic in the air. Literally. Goosebumps raised on my skin, though I was not cold. There was no breeze but my hair floated as if I were swimming in a pool. The scent of cherry blossoms filled the air. I looked to the pinkened sky. Every shade of pink I could imagine and possibly a few more swirled, from the softest pink almost faded to white, to a bright magenta. Because of the lighting the grass and trees took on a rich deep purple hue, and a distant pond looked almost black.

I couldn't believe how light I felt. Like I could fly. Until we started floating, then a panicked look must've crossed my face because Emrys laughed.

"I love when I get to surprise you," he said. Having been there before, he maneuvered himself easily, flying next to me.

"I've seen and done a lot of crazy thing but... flying?" I know I sounded like a child but even Tuatha have dreams of flying. The freedom of actually doing it was exhilarating.

"You'll get the hang of it. Pretty cool isn't it?" He winked. Then he pointed to a distant hill. "We need to cross beyond the ridge. There's a spot next to a large lake. We'll find Druantia there."

I nodded, still amazed that I was flying.

We began slowly until I got the hang of it. I was staying upright, perpendicular to the ground. Emrys leaned forward so he was parallel and I followed. Then we really began to pick up speed. We soared higher up away from the ground. Far higher than the ridge we needed to cross. The distance must've been twenty miles but we traveled so quickly we were there in a matter of minutes.

A large tree with pink blossoms grew next to the lake and under it was a woman. Druantia.

We began our descent and she turned to face us. She was beautiful. Tall and lean. Strong. Long chestnut curls tumbled down past her shoulders and there was a crown of antlers upon her head. Her skin was a porcelain I'd only read about but had never seen the likes of. Large, warm brown eyes were trained on Emrys. Her full pink lips smiled in genuine joy at the sight of him. She wore a forest green gown—the color not only complimented her coloring but starkly contrasted the pink and purple hues of the realm. The low cut of the gown revealed an ample bosom and the snugness of it implied long thin legs.

I couldn't help but glance sideways at Emrys. The Druid looked smitten. Hell, I was smitten at the sight of her. Who could blame him?

"Emrys!" She beamed and embraced him.

He had embraced me thousands of times but not in the way that he embraced Druantia. I felt like I was intruding. To make it more awkward Druantia kissed him with a longing that I well understood. I looked in the other direction at the hills. Seriously, I was staring at hills. I would've done anything to be able to give them some privacy. Regardless, I was going to be grilling Emrys about their history later, because obviously there was a major backstory that I was not aware of.

Emrys finally pried his lips away and spoke, breaking the silence. "Druantia, this is Morrigan."

She released Emrys from her grip and then embraced me as if I were her long lost sister.

Her voice was like honey as she spoke. I could feel the magic in it. Though unlike Emrys, it was unintentional. She was just that powerful that she couldn't hide it. "Morrigan, I feel as though I know you."

"It's an honor to meet you," I managed to say, bowing my head.

"No formality is required here, my dear," she said, releasing me from her embrace but still holding my hand.

She grabbed Emrys' with her other hand and led us to the edge of the lake where we all sat on the soft grass. Mixed into the scent of the cherry blossoms I could smell the moisture from the lake. It was quiet and still, like glass. A breeze fluttered over us.

Druantia's warm eyes stared out over the water. She began, "I get many visitors here. I know many in all the realms. Do you know how many realms there are, Morrigan?"

"Twelve." I answered, not needing to think. Everyone knew that.

Druantia smiled. "Twelve. Twelve that you know of, yes. There are actually fifty-five."

My jaw dropped. I looked to Emrys, his face betrayed that he knew this information already.

Druantia continued, "It is only myself and Emrys now that are left of the Druid Council. We were the only ones who knew how many realms there are. We were in your realm when it was still being created. This is what is left of our realm."

I managed to outwardly compose myself. But only outwardly.

"But our story is a long one. One for another time, I suppose," she said, patting my hand. "Do you know why you can only enter into this realm on Samhain?"

I thought for a moment before answering. "No, I suppose I never gave it any consideration. Only knew it to be the case."

Druantia nodded. "Well let me do my best to explain it." She waved her hand and a small white globe shone bright in the air. Then more colored globes, I'm assuming fifty-five, began to orbit quickly and randomly around the original small white one. It reminded me of seeing someone on a television show Emrys watched once, explaining what an atom looked like.

I stared at the display Druantia created and then she waved her hand and the orbiting slowed down drastically. She pointed to the center globe and said, "This is where The Creator resides. Where he is from. He can and does visit all the realms, and yet he is always there as well." She paused for effect but I was no Emrys. I was not going to try to figure the riddle out. "This is where the Gods of all the realms are from. So it is in effect their home as well."

"I guess I never thought of them as having come from somewhere else," I found myself saying.

Druantia's wise eyes stayed focused on the lake. "They never lived there for any amount of time so one would not think they would imagine it to be home. But then one would be wrong."

Emrys said nothing but he turned from the water to look

at Druantia. She spared him a glance and continued. "You are able to enter here on Samhain and exit here at the exact time the following year because that is the only time, once a year, that our two realms connect. See?"

I looked at the model floating in the air. I could see the small blue orb and the pink orb pass through one another, just the edges brushing together.

"So when our two realms connect, we can enter the realm?" I said, now understanding.

Druantia nodded. "Yes. There are other realms that your realm connects to. Some, like mine, once a year. Others that connect once a century, some daily, and so on. It is not random and since the realms travel around The Creator's realm in various planes it can be eons before some of the realms connect. Some never connect to yours, so you would have to hop from one realm and go into another. Unless you knew to look for them you would never know they existed. Some are still there and are empty, and some never come into contact with your realm, so you are unaware of them."

I kept staring at the model, still in motion. Druantia pointed to a giant globe that swirled black and red. "Watch this one."

The model continued spinning on then slowed down once again. The giant red and black one began to engulf the small blue one, our realm, as a piece of the giant one also transected the small white one, The Creator's.

I didn't understand, but knew that couldn't be good. Emrys and I looked at Druantia, not sure of the impact, and she explained, "The giant red and black one is what humans have come to call Hell. It is where the demons are trapped. The last time the three of these globes intersected was the day of the great battle that you were put into your state of sleep. The day the Gods gathered all the demons they could find and pushed them into that realm."

"Does that mean that the demons can descend upon the

Earthly realm again when this happens? And how much time do we have?" I felt sick at seeing the model continue to move. The black and red globe was twenty times the size of the small blue and white one. It was as if it was taking its time swallowing the bright blue orb as the color faded to an almost black.

"No, and yes I suppose." Druantia didn't waste any time explaining. "It is just the point that they *can* enter your realm. The Gods locked them away. But… they can also unlock it."

I was so confused. "But why would they do that?"

Emrys shook his head and now spoke, "Because they are tired and they want to go home. It's happening again isn't it? They have found a loophole."

Druantia placed her hand upon Emrys' knee and pulled his head to her chest. He let her. I was clueless of what they referred to.

Druantia turned to me and spread her arms, gesturing for me to look at the horizon. "This was once home of all the Druids. Thousands of us. We were very prosperous and busy, visiting other realms, offering our healings and knowledge. Our realm is very, very old. We had been here millions of years. The Gods each passing millennial became more and more complacent. Then they hated us. They wanted to go home. But the only way Gods are allowed to enter the Creator's sphere is if the realm they guard is dead. So they planned an attack and killed every living being. Our realm and three others were destroyed in the span of a day. The other realms were intersecting, the last one touching the Creator's. It was an organized effort of all the Gods of the three realms to strike on the day they were aligned and they essentially hopped from one realm to the other and the other then into the Creator's. The other realms void of Gods are void of life. My magic allows me to keep this place alive but I must remain alone, never leaving, to keep it so. I just cannot bear to leave it and let it die."

My heart ached looking at Emrys and Druantia. I couldn't fathom their loss.

I sat silently, letting Druantia compose herself until she was ready to speak again. "That is where the first great demons came from. The Creator, in his grief and rage at what the Gods had done, turned them into demons and banished them from his home. He made sure that every God in every realm understood that they could not actively be the ones to destroy a realm or this would be their punishment. To eternally be banished and to be hunted down and destroyed by his newest creation, The Tuatha de Danann."

"That is how and why we were created?" I whispered.

Druantia laced her fingers through mine. "Yes. You were meant to bring balance back to the realms. The Gods that were turned to what you call Greater Demons. The Lesser Demons are the beings Greater Demons have twisted and lured into joining them."

I was still in shock but the model stared back at me. I feared I knew the answer but asked anyway. "What does this story have to do with the Hell realm?"

Emrys spoke this time, having pieced the same puzzle together. He looked to Druantia as he spoke for confirmation and she only nodded. "The Gods have found a loophole, like I said. They cannot destroy the realm, otherwise they'll suffer the same fate as their brothers and sisters and be turned into demons. But you see how gigantic that globe is? It will be in contact for seven days with our realm and the Creator's. If the demons were able to destroy the humans in a week's span, on the seventh day, the Gods walk straight through the Hell realm right into the Creator's realm and no rules are broken."

Druantia said, "This plan has been in place for a very long time. Without Tuatha, Druids or Fomoire only the humans would be left, and they would fall quickly."

"That is why we were put to sleep? To be out of the way? But why not destroy us?" I was sounding like Emrys.

"When you found out that the demons were placed in Hell rather than destroyed did that puzzle you?" Druantia asked me.

"Yes, I figured it was the Gods being the Gods. I don't understand a lot of what they do," I answered.

"And instead of destroying you, Artaius had you put to sleep?" she asked.

"Yes, I suppose so,"

Her calculating eyes went from warm to those of a hawk. "There is still much we do not know. I suspect not all the Gods are on board for this plan. The Gods are fickle, though, Morrigan, you are right. Don't trust them. I fear that the war that is coming will be fought on many fronts. Demons and Gods."

I lost my breath at the thought.

"How much time do we have?" Emrys was thinking ahead of me.

"When you return to your realm," she began, "you will have about one and a half years before the Hell realm begins to intersect your realm. It will begin on the spring equinox of that year and as Emrys said, will take seven days."

Her honeyed voice held an edge and urgency to it. "We must raise an army. The Gods will no doubt unlock Hell, and holding the demons back is the only hope we have."

"There are only three hundred of us left," I replied solemnly.

"I know, Morrigan." She stroked my hair as my mother would have. "There is always hope. The Creator will show us a way. I will do what I can on my end to help, and will be with you when Hell comes."

"The Sword of the Tuatha. We need to find it. It was sent away and we don't know where. It's only one sword but…"

Druantia cut me off. "Yes the sword. That is why you really came. To find it. I can help with that."

She stood and so did Emrys and I. She said, "The sword is the only one that can kill a God. Artaius wasn't stupid, though. By binding himself to Arthur, and in turn Arthur binding the sword to him, the sword cannot kill Artaius."

"What?" I shouted.

Druantia put her hands up. "You have one of the descendants of Arthur, correct?"

"Yes, he is training with us," I replied.

"Well then," she said. "That is a simple remedy. He only needs to voluntarily put a single drop of his blood on the sword and freely give it to your King. That is all that it takes to undo that mess."

"Oh, thank the Creator." I finally breathed a sigh of relief. "So where do we find it?"

Druantia's face hardened. "Undoing the bonding is easy enough. There's good news and bad news about where the sword is. First of all, the descendant of Arthur is the only one that can retrieve it. You can go and assist on the quest of course, but he will be the only one they will turn it over to."

"Who are they?" Emrys said cautiously. He seemed to already know the answer.

Druantia sighed. "The Godless."

"Frak! Frack! And frack!" Emrys kicked at the grass as he shouted.

"This is actually a good thing, Emrys." Druantia thickened the honey in her voice.

Emrys came unglued. "A good thing? A good thing? This is a realm that even the Gods fear. This is a realm that nobody knows about because nobody has ever been and returned alive. And you think this is a good thing?"

I was not liking the sound of any of this. I'd never seen Emrys this upset. Not good.

Druantia spoke more firmly to Emrys now. "By the Creator, get yourself under control Emrys, and just listen to me." She turned to me since I had no idea what was going on other than this was going to suck. "Do you know of the Godless, Morrigan?"

"No," I answered truthfully. I was still shocked at there being more than twelve realms. I was having a hard time catching up.

Emrys continued pacing with irritation written on his face. Druantia ignored him and spoke to me. "Word obviously got out to a few of the other realms what had happened when the Gods destroyed my home and the other two realms. The Godless are what you might call a Cyclops?"

"A Cyclops? For real?" I couldn't believe it.

Druantia nodded. "A little different than what your lore would suggest. They have been mostly myth and legends, even to the oldest of realms. They are giants, averaging thirty feet in height. They have one giant bulbous eye and instead of hair, they have long tendrils of flesh sprouting from their heads. Hideous creatures by our standards, but they are not evil."

Emrys interrupted, "Except the whole killing and being eaten part."

Druantia ignored him. "When they heard how the Gods had turned on the realms they feared that the Gods of their realm would do the same. They forged swords that were capable of killing Gods."

"Like The Sword of Tuatha?" I couldn't help interrupting again.

"Yes, that is where the sword came from. But it is just one sword. They had enough for an army. They hunted down and killed all the Gods in their realm. That is why they are called the Godless."

"How does their realm still exist without any Gods?" I asked.

Her voice was musical. "Their realm slowly began to die. No water, no trees or plants. No Gods to keep the world going. It became a vast wasteland. They feed on those who enter from other realms to steal the secret of how to forge the swords. They never enter any other realms because they know a God would risk punishment from the Creator, even being turned into a demon, to kill one of them. Your sword, the Sword of The Tuatha, was given as a gift from their king to your people long ago, when the

Tuatha left your realm to battle demons. The sword not only kills Gods, but the slightest piercing of the skin with it is lethal to the demons as well. Since the higher demons used to be Gods, it works the same."

"You mean to tell me that instead of fighting with regular swords against an army of demons that will only die if you take their head, which is no easy feat, they have swords that will kill demons and Gods with just the piercing of the skin?" I was jubilant. "That is the best news we've gotten."

Druantia smiled. "See! I told you there was good news."

Emrys had to poop on our moment. "And the killing. Don't forget they kill all who enter, then they eat you. Oh, and Druantia, why don't you fill Morrigan in on how it's impossible to get there."

Before my heart could sink Druantia answered him. "It is not impossible. Why, there is someone right now within your very realm that has a stone to enter and a Cup of Plenty to garner an audience with their King."

Emrys looked over his shoulder at her and if there was such a thing as an evil eye he gave it to her. He turned and slowly walked to her. She was a tall woman but he was still much taller. He bent his nose down to her and his voice was sharp. "Even if we can get in. And even giving a Cup of Plenty to the King, there is no guarantee he will give us the sword, or more of them and let us return alive."

"There are no guarantees in life," she said flippantly. "But, a Cup of Plenty would mean a lot to a King in a land with nothing. It would mean drink for all, as much as they could swallow, for eternity. Living on only the blood of the trespassers has made them ravenous. A cup that would never run out, why there is no greater prize. And Emrys, you are very clever. Morrigan, you are the greatest warrior of the Tuatha. You two, upon returning, will take this human descendant of Arthur and go to New York City. The one you seek is frequenting a bar called Blood Moon. There you will find the Cup and stone in their possession. I am unsure who it is. My sources are foggy but I know he is there. That is what I know, and that is what must be done."

Emrys hung his head in defeat. An impossible quest for sure. We had a few of those before, I thought. This blew those all away. We had no choice. No time to develop another plan. No use dwelling on it.

"Your sunset will be here soon." Druantia softly whispered, her lips against Emrys' neck.

I once again turned to the hills. "Emrys, I remember the way back to the Great Oak. I'll meet you there."

The least I could do was let him say goodbye to Druantia properly. This was one journey we might not return from. I flew back to the tree and waited for Emrys, my anticipation at seeing Neil building.

CHAPTER 18

I WAS ON the ground with my back against the tree when I saw Emrys speeding towards me. He descended gracefully, landing gingerly on his feet. I didn't bother teasing him for the goofy grin on his face. Let him enjoy this moment. I couldn't help but raise my eyebrow though, making him laugh.

"I do believe there's quite a story here you will have to tell me about someday," I said as I stood, bumping my hip against him.

"Not gonna happen."

Emrys took my hand and managed to smile even wider. "You ready to get back?"

"I am," I said, smiling back.

We stepped through the Great Oak. Instantly the cool air tickled my face. My heart raced in anticipation as I looked around. King Conall stood alone, holding the reins of his horse and two others. My eyes locked onto his.

King Conall raised one hand as if to say, wait. His voice was warm and calm as he spoke. "Morrigan relax, Neil is fine. Emrys, may I have a private word?"

I heard the words Conall said but my stomach dropped. I knew something had happened. If Neil was 'fine' he would be here. Conall asking to have a private word with Emrys confirmed that something serious had happened and I felt the panic begin to rise within me.

Conall and Emrys stood in front of me. Emrys was having a silent conversation, speaking with Conall in their minds only. Conall kept his eyes trained on me, only glancing at Emrys occasionally. Emrys leapt upon one of the black geldings and raced towards our home. I knew he used magic to enhance the speed because in an instant he was out of sight.

"Conall, I'm terrified. Neil is not fine. Tell me this instant. What's happened?" I pleaded.

Conall tied the reins of both horses to a tree then walked to me. He was slow, methodical, and calm. Fear bubbled under my skin.

Gently taking my hands in his, he bent over, kissing my cheek. His eyes were soft. The look on his face was one I hadn't seen in centuries. Without knowing it, that look, conveyed to me what had happened. I bent over, gasping for air as if having been punched in the gut by a giant. That would have been less painful. I dropped to my knees.

Conall knelt next to me. He put one hand on my back then pulled me to his chest and I buried my face into him. He began, "About three months after you had gone Brian came to me with some suspicions. I put Aiden on task of rooting out the truth."

I silently cried into Conall's chest. Tears streamed down my face and without looking he used his thumb to brush them from my cheek.

I managed to catch my breath and said, "Go on."

Conall cleared his throat. "Riley—the Druid girl that Emrys asked to take charge and continue the trainings—she and the others were being integrated into working with the Knights as a team. She and Neil... Well, there was an attraction."

I tried to take a deep calming breath but it hitched in my throat. My voice sounded shaky as I said, "So he's with her now. Almost as soon as I was gone, he was with her."

Conall said nothing. It wasn't a question. It was a statement. One I knew to be true. My heart ached as if it had been carved from my still breathing body. At the same time, I felt a wrath deep inside me at having been discarded so easily. So quickly. My anger didn't stop at him. I couldn't believe that I was so foolish. How could I have been so blind? Again?

Conall picked me up in his arms, walking me over to the horses. He put me down so I could stand, placing his hands on both sides of my face. Piercing my eyes with his he spoke as forcefully and regally as I'd ever heard. "We are going to go back. Emrys is beginning a Samhain celebration the likes that no one has ever seen. We are going to begin the feast as is *our* duty and enjoy this night. I cannot tell you how sorry I am for what has happened. You know, I... I..."

I put my fingers to Conall's lips. I stopped crying and said, "You needn't say any more, my King. I will be composed by the time we arrive. I was taken by surprise is all." I hesitated. "I'll be fine."

Conall gave me his little crooked smile and bowed. "To the celebration, then."

CHAPTER 19

I KEPT TRUE to my word. I composed myself by the time we arrived. Conall caught me up on Treasach, Alastar and Aine and I couldn't wait to see them. My heart was heavy in my chest and my gut felt like an empty pit. I could not control how I felt but I could control how I acted. Barely.

We made good time as we rode towards the stables. I expected to see people but none were to be found.

Conall smiled and winked. "Everyone will be on the back lawn. Emrys no doubt has everything ready and is just waiting on us."

"That's precisely correct, Your Majesty," Emrys boomed as he appeared from nowhere.

We both dismounted our horses and turned them loose in the pasture.

Emrys gave me one of his famous bear hugs. I looked at him and smiled. I was hurt, but I wouldn't show it tonight. Tonight I was going to enjoy my people. My family. The fate of our realm still hung in uncertainty. These celebrations were to be reminders to enjoy the moments, the time that we did have.

Emrys pulled back and rubbed his fingers on his chin. "We're going full on traditional tonight." Then he snapped his fingers.

I felt a gush of air whip at me and as quick as it came on,

it fled. I felt myself off balance and I realized I was no longer wearing my boots.

"Here let me help cure your curiosity," Emrys said, placing a reflection spell in front of me.

I stood staring into the 'mirror' that Emrys had created. I wore a gown of gold, actual spun gold, that clung and flowed. It was like the one my mother had been crowned Queen in. I remember thinking the first time I saw it as a child that it was the most beautiful piece of clothing that had ever been created. I still held that belief. It was amazing.

"Oh Emrys it's… I'm breathless," I said softly.

"You make us all breathless," Conall whispered. I saw his reflection as he walked up behind me. He wore a golden breastplate with ornate knot work and dragon carved upon it. His trousers, boots, everything, gold just like my gown.

He gently ran his hands over the soft curls that hung down my back. Emrys had woven an ornate braid, pulling the hair around my face back into a half updo. I had worn my hair like this many times before. I smiled knowing why he had my hair fixed like this.

"Shall we?" Emrys led the way from the stables.

We turned the corner but before we could make our way to the back lawn where the party would be we stopped. I could hear voices but it looked completely black. Not even any modern lights were on.

Treasach, Alastar and Aine stood smiling at seeing King Conall, Emrys and myself come around the corner. Treasach's gold breastplate had the stag carved into it while Alastar's had the bull. Fitting for both of them. Aine's golden mermaid style gown was velvet and her hair wound up high upon her head. I noticed Deidra standing next to Aine and she made her way to me.

Deidra was one of the most stunning women I'd ever laid eyes upon. I could see why she held the King's eye. She wore a gown of silver and her platinum hair rippled with every step she took. She stopped short of me and bowed. She raised her head and for the first time since we've known one another, looked me in the eye and spoke with no edge. "Morrigan, I have no words for the loss you have endured today. For the loss you have endured in your past. I am truly sorry. I cannot right what has been wronged. I have never told you that because of fear. Fear that I would lose the love of the King. But I am sorry."

I was truly taken aback at how genuinely she spoke. I grabbed her hand and squeezed knowingly. I didn't dare speak, I had a lump in my throat that threatened to escape.

"Well let's get this show started," Emrys said with a twinkle in his eye.

I couldn't see Emrys. Myself, King Conall, Treasach, Alastar, Aine and Deidra were suspended above the roof of the residence. There wasn't a light to be seen. A magic veil held even the moon's light. I felt a weight upon my head and I smiled.

Emrys had no need for a sound system. I knew not where he was but his voice boomed over the crowd. "Tuatha, Druids and Knights. We are gathered here in celebration of Samhain. To give thanks for a plentiful year! To feast! Together we will battle and prevail over evil. This night though, is for festivities. I give to you, your royal family!"

The crowd cheered. A spotlight of candlelight illuminated us. My eyes adjusted and I looked at Conall. His crown sat regally upon his head. While his was thick, it was not tall. Mine was thin and ornate and very tall. The weight of it was more than I remembered.

King Conall took my hand and we began to proceed down the invisible staircase leading us to the ground. Blackness still blanketed the crowd, and I could see no one.

"King Conall and Queen Morrigan," Emrys announced as we touched the ground.

Then as one by one descended he continued, "Prince Treasach… Prince Alastar… Princess Aine… Lady Deidra."

The crowd cheered at the announcement of each name. I could also catch the gasps and confusion from the Druids and Knights who were unaware I was Queen. They continued cheering as we made our way down the lawn towards the large pile of wood for the lighting of the bonfire ceremony. Emrys hadn't disappointed, and even though the grounds were still shrouded in darkness I could tell by the crushed red velvet carpet under my feet even I was going to be wowed tonight.

I glanced at Conall, he looked every bit the King he was. He must've read my mind as he said, "You look regal as ever, my Queen."

I was more comfortable leading the Teulu. I had been Queen for over five hundred years. Well over five hundred years, before we went into our slumber, that is. I was never comfortable in ceremonies such as these and always pretended to be my mother. She acted and looked like a queen at all times. I kept my shoulders back. I glided in long strides, keeping my head high, never letting my crown slip. Just like she taught me.

I picked Emrys' voice out of the crowd. It was in his regular tone, not the one he projected to the crowd. He was close, speaking to an observer. Conall heard it too. Though neither of us glanced in the direction of the conversation, Conall gave my hand a squeeze at hearing it, and out of the corner of my eye I saw a tiny grin creep up on his face.

I heard Neil first. "Queen Morrigan?"

Emrys chuckled then said, "Did you not know that, boy?"

"No." Neil sounded as if he were in shock. "But Deidra? I thought she was the King's wife?"

Emrys answered, "Nope. Your marriage ceremonies are similar to the Tuatha. Till death do you part. Except the Tuatha take vows very seriously. They live much, much longer than you

humans so it isn't unheard of for a married couple to live separate
love lives, but the bond of marriage still remains."

Neil said nothing but Emrys paused for effect then continued.
"Conall and Morrigan were both Teulu and fought together side
by side for a century when they fell in love. You know how it
goes. Got married, had kids, then..."

"Kids?" Neil interrupted.

"Well yeah. Treasach, Alastar and Aine. Hell, Aine looks
almost identical to Morrigan. Did you never notice?" Emrys was
egging him on. "Treasach looks a lot like his father but Alastar
strongly resembles Morrigan's father."

Neil was still confused. "But Deidra?"

Emrys was kind in his answer, no doubt because he knew we
were listening. After the way Deidra had greeted me upon my
return I had softened towards her and let any animosity that
still lingered go. "Morrigan and Daur were on a quest and were
caught in another realm fighting a war for over a century. When
she returned, the King had found comfort with Deidra and had
fallen in love with her. He thought Morrigan dead, having been
gone that long."

"So he chose Deidra?" Neil asked.

Emrys replied, "He waited one hundred years before he
accepted Morrigan's death. And chose Deidra after Morrigan
returned? That's not at all what I said."

Silence, then Emrys said, "Gotta go, things to do and all."

My heart panged at hearing Emrys recount my return to find
Conall was with Deidra. I understood Conall had waited. I had
no way to get back home or send word to him and fought as
hard as I could to return. I sympathized with Deidra. No matter
how hurt I was to see Conall with her. I knew that if I said that
I wanted him to be with me, even though he cared for her very
much, he would return in an instant, even now. She knew it as
well, and I felt sorry for her for that.

Conall and I made our way to the end of the carpet. Emrys was now off to the side and nodded at the King.

King Conall spoke, commanding the crowd. "I am pleased that the full royal family is here in celebration of Samhain. Queen Morrigan has returned with good news. Our Queen, always finding... no, creating... creating hope, even when hope seems lost. She is our shining light. Tomorrow she will lead yet another quest to save the realm. But tonight, we celebrate!"

I bowed to King Conall, as did our children, Deidra, and the rest of the crowd. Conall, Deidra, the children and myself stood and faced the bonfire to be lit. We raised our hands, and using the bit of magic we had, shot flames into the large woodpile. With a *whoosh* a twenty story bonfire ignited. The crowd stood and cheered.

Emrys took over from there. The large bonfire's flames danced and jumped, lighting up other, smaller bonfires that hung high up in the air. The sky was alight and the smoky scent warmed the air. Tables heaped with roasted meats, baskets of bread and herbed vegetables lined the lawn. Music filled the air and mugs of ale welcomed everyone to their seats.

We took our place at the head table. I took the throne to the King's right, Deidra sitting on his left. Treasach, Alastar and Aine sat to my right. I allowed myself to feel the joy of having my family and friends with me. To not let Neil, who thought so little of me that I was replaced after a few months, ruin my evening. I refused to let him ruin one moment of my life. Any grieving I did at the Great Oak would be the only grieving I would do. At least that's what I told myself.

I looked at Deidra. She gave me a warm smile. We had come to an understanding, she and I. I simply nodded my thanks. I knew the King loved her. I knew he loved me as well. He had room for both of us in his heart. At times I wished I could live with that. I was not made that way, though.

I enjoyed every bite of the feast and every ounce of the ale

I drank. Emrys and I shared a few glances, knowing it would be a long while before we enjoyed festivities again. I caught the King up on what Druantia had shared with us and what must be done. He was not pleased, but as King, knew the quest was our only hope.

Conall leaned towards me to say softly, "Are you up for leaving tomorrow at sunset with Emrys and Neil, or do you need more time?"

I'd stuck to the promise I made myself about remaining composed and answered, "There is no more time, my King. I am fine."

Conall nodded towards Daur. "Looks like your old friend is ready for a dance. Go enjoy this night."

And I did.

CHAPTER 20

THE SAMHAIN CELEBRATION lasted until sunrise. Once the sun came up we made our way back to our rooms. King Conall had taken it upon himself to have my stuff moved to a different room. I appreciated the gesture. No need to have old memories try to pull at me if it could be avoided.

I awoke in the strange room, taking a moment to remember where I was. The shades were drawn to keep the daylight out, but by midafternoon the light was winning, and I pulled myself from the featherbed.

Glad that I had slept so soundly and had a wonderful evening with friends and family I put my leathers on. I stared in the mirror as I braided my hair and wound it tight on top of my head. I put my two medium swords and longsword into their sheaths on my back. Two short knives went into each boot.

The residence was eerily quiet. I ate and made my way to the library. I was shocked to see Neil there and my skin pricked as the adrenalin shot through me.

He looked up at me and began, "Listen, Morrigan I just want to say how sorry I am. I…"

I cut him off. "No apologies, Neil, they're pointless. Apologies are only to make the asshole feel better. Not the one that was wronged. If it's forgiveness you seek, ask the Creator. You won't get it from me."

"Wow." He shook his head. "I understand you're upset. I never meant to—"

Again I cut him off. With no emotion in my eyes or voice I said, "Neil, what's done is done. There is no need to speak about this any further. The fate of the realm rests on us succeeding in this impossible task. Let's just focus on that."

Thankfully Emrys walked in, followed by Conall. I was relieved to not be alone with Neil, but the tension rose as the King stopped an inch from Neil and looked down at him. The King looked more like a lethal warrior than a leader at the moment. He was menacing.

His voice was slow and though it was even, the edge in it was apparent. "You are an insignificant worm. If you were not necessary to this quest, I would drive my sword into you a thousand times. When this is done, you need to make sure you stay clear of me, or I will."

Neil looked defiantly up at the King, not backing down. "And Riley and our unborn child? While I'm gone will you harm them?"

The air thickened with tension. I saw Conall's jaw tense though his expression hadn't changed. It took all my control to keep my face from reacting. The food I had just eaten churned. Outwardly I remained stoic. I looked at Emrys. He fidgeted with his fingernail the way he always did when he wanted to appear calm.

The King smiled. This was definitely his 'Relax, I'm not going to kill you right now but when I can I will and I will do it painfully' smile. His voice dropped barely above a whisper. This was a warning and Neil knew it. "I wouldn't touch the woman and child. But this changes nothing between you and I."

Emrys broke the tension before Neil could reply, surely escalating the situation. "Okay, everyone here has a big cock, wonderful. Mine is the biggest. The Blood Moon opens at nine Eastern time. No need to get there right away. Why don't we all just enjoy the rest of the day? We'll meet in the stables at eight. Be dressed in battle gear."

Neil headed out the door. The King, Emrys and I stayed behind. Emrys said, "Well damn, Morrigan. You not only got cheated on, he got the girl knocked up. You could go on Springer."

I laughed at the reference. "You know I have to laugh to keep from crying. This is ridiculously messed up."

The King's mood had lightened as well. "I did *not* see that coming."

We poured a drink and laughed. The jovial mood reminded me of simpler times, when I was just a warrior with no personal life that complicated things.

"I'm going to spend the rest of the day with the children. Conall, I'll come see you before we head to the Great Oak," I said as I walked out.

CHAPTER 21

BRIAN AND DAUR accompanied us on the ride to the Great Oak. Daur kept us entertained with his lively stories. Without him we surely would have ridden in silence.

We dismounted and I handed the reins to them.

"Brian, I'm not sure how long we'll be. Pray the Creator we're back in time. Continue trainings and counsel the King in my absence," I said then turned to Daur. "You keep my children ready. You hear me?"

He laughed and kissed my hand. "Anything for you, my Queen." Then he picked me up and hugged me.

"Okay, let's do this," Emrys said, standing next to Neil.

I took the lead and walked through the Great Oak. Emrys took Neil's arm and led him through.

We exited into New York City. We were in a park. It was dark but still there were people about.

"Emrys, mirage," I barked.

"Done," he replied.

"What's that all about?" Neil asked, turning to me.

"We're decked out in leathers and swords. The humans will see us as just three forgettable figures walking through the streets. I can create my own mirage but Emrys needs to create yours," I answered.

We walked to The Blood Moon, less than a mile away. I was

amazed at how vast the city seemed. I had seen it on television of course, but experiencing it was a wonder I wasn't prepared for. Standing across the street we could see a line of humans waiting to get in that wound around the building. It seemed a seedy part of town to have this large a crowd. There were no other businesses open in the area. From the outside it looked to be a large warehouse. The Blood Moon sign was in neon, offering the only color on the grey façade.

The music could be heard from the outside. Techno. It was awful. I dreaded having to walk in and hear it at full volume. Hopefully the smell would be better, because the street reeked of garbage, urine and filth.

We walked to the doorman, cutting in line. There were some yells from the crowd but Emrys got us in without incident.

Inside the music thumped. Years of alcohol being sloshed onto the floor and rarely cleaned permeated the air. It was dark with only red lights illuminating the large space. The place was massive. There was an area with a long bar that had at least twenty bartenders. In front of the bar, couches and chairs were filled with people partying. The dance floor was the size of our great dining hall and was elbow to elbow with people dancing.

Emrys shouted as loud as he could to me, "How are we going to find a person we don't even know in this crowd?"

"Let's go to the bar and get a drink. I'll figure something out." I winked

We made our way through the crowd. The closer we got to the bar the more it became apparent. Emrys and I shared a glance.

Neil noticed. "What? What's wrong?"

I answered, "The bartenders are all vampires."

Neil mumbled. "Now what?"

"Like I said, let's get a drink." I shrugged.

Of course Emrys had to know I knew the answer to his question so I assume he asked for Neil's sake. "You realize the mirage won't work on vampires. They will see us in leathers and with swords."

"Uh huh," I replied.

"Sometimes I ask myself why I always come with you on these quests. I suppose I'm a glutton for punishment." Emrys rolled his eyes as he spoke.

"It's because I'm great fun." I smiled.

My head pounded with the bass. How anyone could spend hours in this place on purpose for fun was beyond me.

One of the vampire bartenders saw us before we could get to the bar. He said something to a couple of the others. One scurried off and the other two came out from behind the bar to meet us.

The shorter of the two vampires said, "We know who you are. You've been hunting our kind for the past year. You're fools for coming here."

Before I could reply there were eight other vampires surrounding us.

The smug short one spoke again, "You're outmatched this time. Our King has told us what you are. Tuatha? Is that what you're called?"

They all laughed. I kept my face placid, as did Emrys. I could see Neil seething but he followed our lead and kept calm.

"There are only three of you. You won't make it out of here alive. But before we kill you I'm going to take you to our King. He may want to question you first," he said with a smug grin. Then he leaned in and poked his fangs out. "Once he's done with you, I will drain you personally."

We still said nothing. I enjoy the witty banter between two rivals in movies, but in reality it's best to say nothing. Take their head when you can.

"Don't make a scene, and follow me. If you make one wrong move we'll kill you," he said, looking at Emrys this time.

Emrys played with his fingernail and nodded.

We wound through the crowd to the back where there was a staircase roped off. Two werewolves guarded it.

I raised an eyebrow at Emrys. He spoke in my mind. "Well I guess you got us the audience with their King that we'd been looking for. Still doesn't get us any closer to finding the clown we need to meet in order to get us to the Godless. I hope you know what you're doing."

I was winging it, of course. Praying that whomever we were supposed to find might find us. Hopefully we would live long enough for that to happen.

The werewolves kept their eyes trained on us. Though they were in human form I could see the hair on the back of their necks rise. They wanted to take our throats but showed restraint. They followed orders.

We climbed stairs that opened up into a waiting room of sort. The carpet was red and the walls gilded, covered in Baroque artwork. At the other end were large double doors, the golden handles shaped like serpents. It was ostentatious and gaudy.

The short one turned and ordered, "Remove your weapons. And no tricks."

"No," I replied.

He looked stunned. They looked at one another, unsure of what to do.

I could feel the challenged ego of the vampire flare. He stepped closer, baring his fangs at me. "Bitch I said remove your weap—"

Before he could finish his sentence I unsheathed one of my shorter swords and took his head. The others hesitated. Before they could react and this ended in disaster, I placed it back into the sheath and said, "We will not remove our weapons, but as guests we will wait to see your King." I took two steps to the black leather couch and sat.

Emrys nonchalantly sauntered over and sat next to me, grabbing a magazine off the table. Neil shook his head, gathering his wits, and walked over to the couch, tripping over his foot once.

One of the vampires went through the double doors. The rest stood on the balls of their feet waiting for us to attack. Occasionally they would look at the pile of ashes their friend had disintegrated into.

I kept my face blank but was on alert. I knew Emrys was as well, but he was flipping through the magazine. He broke the silence by ripping out a page. I looked at him as if he were insane.

He shrugged. "It's a recipe for jambalaya and it looks really good."

I looked over at Neil to gauge how he was holding up. He looked tense and was forcing himself to remain still. I could sense he wanted to draw his sword and start fighting. He was young and inexperienced, he needed to learn patience.

The double doors opened. When I saw who walked through, my blank mask dropped for a second and I struggled to replace it. Cian, son of the King of the Fomoire. My ultimate nemesis.

Emrys was folding the recipe he had torn out and placing it in his pocket. His eyes bugged out for a moment then he looked at me. I only shrugged.

He spoke into my mind. "What the frak?"

I couldn't help it, a small smile pulled at one side of my mouth.

Cian strode across the room as if he were greeting dinner guests. He was as tall as Emrys. I've known him hundreds of years and faced him many times in battle. He was smart and fierce and arguably better with a sword than me. I'd never been able to defeat him, only escape, hoping to live another day to take his head.

He wore black trousers that flowed down his long legs and a black shirt that covered his lean muscles. The last time I saw him his black hair came to his shoulders. The day of the great battle before we were put into our long sleep. It was now cut short, making his sharp jawline more prominent.

He smiled warmly as he approached. We all rose from the

couch. Cian extended his hand to me, his ice blue eyes bored into mine as he said, "Hello there, long lost friend. Long lost enemy. I am nothing more than a memory."

The words. The words that were there when Emrys had been released from the long sleep. The words I had memorized and poured over hundreds of times. The words left by the person who awoke Emrys. The words from the one who had saved us. He was the one we were to find.

I felt Emrys open a communication connection between us. I let him.

Cian shook my hand, and in it placed something. I needn't look. I could tell what it was. It was a stone. It was *the* stone. The one that would get us into the land of the Godless.

I took my hand away and put it in my pocket, keeping the stone safe. I could feel Emrys and Neil staring at me. I couldn't peel my eyes from Cian's. I couldn't move.

"Morrigan, does any of this make sense? Is Cian helping us or helping to kill us? He's the guy we're supposed to find? Does any of this make sense to you?" Emrys said into my mind.

I was still recovering from seeing him. I couldn't reply to Emrys.

I felt Neil sense something was off, but he remained poised.

Cian said, without looking away from me, "Please come in. The King would like to speak with you."

We followed Cian. The remainder of the vampires followed us in.

The King sat at a desk at the far end of the long room. Like the garish décor of the lobby, it was large and ornately carved. Shelves were lined with rare artifacts and it looked more like a museum than an office.

Four werewolves were on each side of the King. They looked like statues flanking their master. The King stayed seated. He was handsome. His olive skin, dark hair and sharp features made me think him to be of Italian descent. He had on an expensively tailored grey suit with a blood red tie that stood out against his crisp starched white shirt. He looked like one would imagine a vampire King would. I wondered to myself if he poured over every vampire movie ever made to make sure he looked the part, or if he created this look of his own accord.

He spoke and I'll be damned if it wasn't in an Italian accent. "You have killed many, many of our kind. Why do you come here today? Are you here to kill more of us?"

We stood four feet away from his desk. There were no chairs between us. Cian leaned against a shelf next to one of the werewolves. The vampires stayed back by the door. There were no windows. Emrys, Neil and myself were trapped in a room with a vampire King, seven vampires, eight werewolves, and the greatest Fomoire warrior that ever lived. The situation was bleak, to say the least.

"We came here for a drink, actually," I answered. "We were unaware that this was your place, or that vampires and werewolves would be crawling all over it."

His dark brown eyes were furious, though he showed no expression on his face. He might be a very old vampire, but I wagered I was older. He was not as practiced at masking his thoughts as I was.

His smile was disingenuous. "You say you came here for a drink? I think you came here to kill me. My Prime has taught me all about you Tuatha. You are arrogant and think yourselves to be better than us, but that's where you're wrong. There aren't that many of you, and we are many. More than you can imagine. We were unprepared before, but now we are not. You will no longer hunt us down."

The King paused before continuing his seemingly well-rehearsed speech. Cian pulled two samurai swords off the wall, one with each hand, and took the heads of the four werewolves he was standing next to in two fluid slashes.

He looked at me and yelled, "Get the wolves before they shift! Emrys, wall!"

Emrys created a magical wall between us and the vampires that had guarded the door. They dashed forward and smacked into it. I pulled my shorter swords and was on the wolves, Neil at my side.

I slashed through the neck of the werewolf closest to me. Black blood squirted out all over me as his body turned to ash. The wolf next to him lunged at me, beginning to shift. I stabbed both swords into his chest, keeping him from reaching me, as Neil used his sword to behead him.

Though Neil and I worked well as a team, we were not quick enough. The two werewolves remaining had time to shift. They were as massive as I remembered the ones in New Orleans to be. The lifeless, blood red eyes looked at me as their lips curled up over the large canines. One let out a howl. A warning to the others.

The larger of the wolves jumped at Neil and me. We parted. The wolves were smart. They were trying to separate us. Neil now stood next to Emrys. I found myself next to Cian. The King stayed out of the fight but did finally get out of his chair. He had his back against the wall.

I aimed one sword at Cian and the other at the werewolf.

Cian rolled his eyes then readied his swords at the wolf. He grinned as he said, "Really Morrigan? You couldn't fight both of us at the same time. You know I would win." He paused and grinned even wider. "Lucky for you I'm here to save you."

My anger swelled but I fell in beside Cian. The wolf leapt at us. Cian and I separated so the wolf was between us. We drove our swords deep into its side. The wolf didn't react. If he felt pain he didn't show it. His large mouth seemed to unhinge, making it abnormally wide, and bit at me. I swung one of my swords through his neck. I misjudged how tough he was. The sword only made it halfway through and stuck. I used the other sword to stab through the other side. He moved quickly so it barely pierced him. His teeth steadily gnashed at me. My right hand was on the sword lodged halfway through his neck and I was working the sword in my left hand trying to get a shot, any shot, at the other side of his neck. I needed leverage but I couldn't get far enough back without letting go with my right hand. The second I did that, he would have his teeth in my neck.

I looked back to see if Emrys could be of any help. Neil was steadily landing shots with his long sword into the wolf they were battling, but like this one, it didn't slow nor show any pain. Emrys had his sword out, making no more headway than Neil.

Cian appeared on the back of the beast I faced. He stood as if he were king of the mountain looking down at my struggle. The teeth were getting closer as I was losing ground. The heat from the beast's breath radiated onto my face. It smelled of rotten flesh.

Cian seemed to enjoy the predicament. "Would you like my help now, love?"

"Yes, now would be good," I answered impatiently.

Cian twirled his sword a few times then winked. His cocky grin melted into the hardened lines I was used to seeing. He gripped the hilt of his sword with both hands and swung with all of his strength. The head was severed. Gallons of black blood gushed over me as I fell onto my back. My hands were still on my swords. The body of the wolf turned to ash.

I was about to stand up when Cian appeared, standing gallantly in front of me. Not a drop of blood on him nor a hair out of place. He extended his hand to help me up.

I was about to accept it, worn from struggling so long when he said, "I'm a sucker for a damsel in distress."

I put my hand on the ground and kicked my leg out, sweeping his legs from beneath him. He landed hard on his back. Right in the ashes.

I stood and muttered, "You're a douchebag," to Cian. He laughed and sat up, dusting himself off.

I turned to help Emrys and Neil to see them standing above a pile of ash as well. We had defeated the werewolves.

The vampire King stood motionless. I'm sure he was hoping we had forgotten about him. The other vampires, still behind the invisible wall Emrys had put up, pounded helplessly, trying to save their King. Or just to kill us. Probably a little of both.

I was soaked in the black ooze and the smell of sulfur and death curled my nose. Emrys walked up to me, shaking his head.

"I know this is the only reason you ask me to come on these outings with you," he said, snapping his fingers, returning me to my clean self.

Cian walked up next to me and said, "Brother how about a little help for me? I'm covered in werewolf ash. It's disgusting."

Emrys glared at Cian and retorted, "It suits you."

Neil stood next to Emrys. He only had a few drops of the blood on him. He looked at me. "Are you okay, Morrigan?"

"She is, thanks to me," Cian answered for me.

Before Cian could unnerve me I turned my attention to the vampire King and raised my sword to his neck. "Emrys, can you take his memories?"

"Let's see," he answered, walking to the vampire.

"You will die. You will all die. You have no idea how powerful the Prime is. You can kill me but he will defeat you in the end. We are his creation." The vampire was beginning to panic.

I had both swords to his neck crisscrossing each other, one on each side. Emrys placed his hands on the vampire's head. Both of their eyes went white. No matter how many times I'd seen this done it gave me the creeps.

Cian looked at the invisible wall holding the other vampires back. The door that we entered into the room was now open. Werewolves and vampires were piling in. The arrogance had left his voice as he said, "We need to hurry and get out of here." He turned to me. "You still have the stone?"

I nodded, looking between Emrys and the invisible wall.

Hoping that he could manage to hold it while sifting the memories of the vampire.

The seconds dragged but the color returned to their eyes and the connection broke. Emrys stepped back and nodded to me.

Without hesitation I removed the vampire's head.

Neil let out a small involuntary gasp. I suppose he wasn't expecting it. The vampires and werewolves were in a frenzy and were piling on top of one another from floor to ceiling trying to get through the wall.

Cian broke the silence. "We need to get out of here. Emrys, any chance you can blast through this back wall? It will open up to the outside of the building. We can hoof it from there."

Emrys looked insulted. "You know damn well I can blast through this wall. But the better question is why in the hell do you think I'm going to let a Fomoire come with us?"

Cian's temper danced around the edges of his icy eyes as he said, "By the Creator I saved you, Emrys. I found a way to raise you so that you could raise the Tuatha. We don't have time to go into all of this right now. I'll tell you what I know when we don't have a few hundred vampires and werewolves waiting to rip us to shreds."

Emrys was close to losing his temper as well, gauging by the steel in his voice. "You might have saved us, but I *know* you, Cian. It was for your own gain. I don't know what it is yet that you want. But I know with everything that I am that you have an angle you're working. You gave Morrigan the stone. Give us the Cup of Plenty and we'll be on our way."

Cian's cocky grin returned. He rubbed his hands over the stubble of his square jaw. He unbuttoned the cuffs of his sleeve. His eyes twinkled as he said, "Geez, Emrys I'd love to do that and all but oh wait..."

He rolled his right sleeve up to his elbow. On his forearm was the tattoo of a chalice.

He continued, "Looks like the Cup of Plenty has been

magically tucked away, to be released by me only when I see fit. And I think I will see it fit when we're in the land of the Godless."

Emrys' eyes bugged out of his head. "Who said anything about going to the land of the Godless?"

My swords were drawn in an instant as were Neil's. We stayed ready.

Emrys said, "We knew we were to find someone here who had the stone and the Cup of Plenty. But how did you know our plan? We only just came up with it."

Cian had perfected the half grin he gave. I'm sure every woman he met melted at it. I wanted to smack it off his face. He acted as though he didn't have swords within inches of his neck. He answered, "You have your ways, I have mine. You think Druantia is the only enlightened one in all the realms? While she may have told you to come find the person with the stone and cup. I have *my* source that said I would need to free you. By the way, why did it take you so long to awaken the Tuatha?" He shook his head for effect. The asshole. He went on, "And that when all the pieces were in place the Tuatha would seek me out so that we can go on a great adventure to the Godless. That way we can get the swords and build an army and defeat the evil and all live happily ever after."

The man made my skin crawl. He was condescending and above all else, I didn't trust him. He would betray us and kill us at his first opportunity. But we had no choice.

I ordered, "Emrys blast a hole in the wall. We make a run for the Great Oak and enter the land of the Godless. He's coming with us, apparently."

Neither Neil nor Emrys protested. Cian looked defiantly at Emrys as if he'd won.

I stepped so close to Cian that an outsider might think we were about to kiss. I looked up into his eyes and quietly vowed, "I will not hesitate to kill you, Cian. Do not give me reason."

His face appeared genuine, with no smugness present as he

answered, "I swear to you Morrigan, Queen of Tuatha, I will not betray you or your people. I am at your service."

The fact was, he appeared to be telling the truth. His being so genuine unnerved me. I couldn't tell when the man was lying.

Emrys blasted a hole into the wall behind the vampire King's desk. He grabbed Neil and jumped out of the second story into the ally. Cian and I turned to see the vampires and werewolves leave the invisible wall and race out the door. We jumped into the alley.

"We're gonna have company in a minute. Can you give Neil speed to keep up?" I asked Emrys.

"Done." He said in a flick of his wrist.

The four of us raced towards the Great Oak. The streets were empty except for a few people and we no longer had our mirage. Though a few hundred vampires and werewolves barreling behind us I suppose would draw more attention than the four of us.

I was thankful Emrys had given Neil increased speed. I only hoped it would last. I was pushing myself past my own limits. I didn't risk looking back. I didn't need to. I could feel them close behind us.

Cian yelled between his gasps for air. "Emrys, one more favor to ask. Think you can recall what my battle gear looked like and could help a fella out now?"

Emrys boomed, "You are out of favors today but seeing as how we may need to fight our way through this, I'll do this for *us* not you."

He flung his hand and Cian was dressed as I had always remembered him. Gone were the modern clothes and shoes. He wore the strange mixture of black leather with the darkest blue fish scales. I knew the Fomoire all wore this, as an homage to the seas in which they ruled. Cian like most Fomoire had the blackest of hair and blue eyes. The coloring complimented him, and he knew it. His boots were black and lined full of knives. His long sword was fastened to his back and his whip curled onto his hip. Besides his hair being shorter and his stubble at the perfect length due to modern beard trimmers, he looked the way I remembered. Lethal.

Cian spoke as we ran. "Morrigan, you have the stone. You will need to go in first. We all need to be holding hands to enter the land of the Godless. If we break contact, even for a second, anyone other than Morrigan will be lost between realms."

Neil tried unsuccessfully to keep the concern from his voice. "What does that mean?"

Cian's sense of humor had returned, "I just told you dumbass. Where did you find this guy?"

"Shut up!" I ordered.

We were nearing the Great Oak. We should have been relieved to see it but our hopes were sunk in an instant. In front of the Great Oak were at least a hundred vampires. I glanced back as we ran. Though there were more vampires than werewolves, the werewolves were all behind us. They were far more deadly.

I formulated a plan. "Emrys, can you put a barrier up behind us? Cian and I will fight through the vampires to get us to the Great Oak."

Emrys didn't look insulted I was asking about his skill and ability. He was calculating if he could do it. "I can't put up a wall but what I can do is create a bubble. A cage around us and the vampires in front of us with the Great Oak inside as well. I will have to focus on keeping the bubble intact. Neil, you will have to fend off any vampires that get near me while Morrigan and Cian take out the rest."

We were getting close, this was going to have to work. Neil spoke up, "Morrigan and Cian can't take out that many vampires. I've gone on dozens of missions to clear vampire nests. Two can't defeat that many. I need to help."

Cian spoke up, "You haven't much faith in us have you boy?"

We were only yards away. I put as much firmness into my

voice as I could. "Neil, do as you're told. Protect Emrys. Do not let any vampires that may get past Cian and I live."

"Morrigan you'll die!" Neil pleaded.

My heart ached for half a beat. I didn't know if his concern was really for me or for us all to get out of this situation. Once, I would have thought it to be because he cared about me.

Cian laughed as we slowed down and turned to me, "He's never seen you fight has he?"

"I've seen her fight plenty asshole. This is a suicide mission." Neil spat.

"Easy boys I need to focus." Emrys said. His face held determination and calmness. I was enamored at how he was able to put himself in such a state when there was so much chaos around. He threw his hands up and electricity hit the air and sparked. A large bubble enclosed us. Emrys stayed at the farthest point away from the Great Oak, holding up the shield. Hundreds of werewolves and vampires hit it but it held. They clawed, bit and kicked at it. I knew Emrys was working hard and that this wouldn't hold forever. The vampires in front of the Great Oak were confused but only for a moment.

I turned to Neil, "I mean it. Anything that gets past us you kill it. Emrys can't take his focus away for a moment or we're all dead."

Neil's eyes were soft as he looked into mine. A look I'd seen so many times and never took for granted. It hurt to have him look at me now. He nodded and spoke, "I promise Morrigan. I promise I will. But you..."

"Oh God...this is absolutely awful and pathetic." Cian interrupted. "Sit back and watch how the grownups do it. She'll be fine. She's got me!" He shot Neil a spectacularly white toothy grin.

Neil's eyes slanted but before he could say anything the vampires started to advance.

"OK Cian, let's see if you have gotten rusty over the years.

I was only asleep. You have been sitting around getting fat and hanging out with vampires." I said pulling my swords.

"Red, try to keep up." He winked.

The vampires stopped short of us. One in the center spoke. "You will pay for what you have done!"

I looked to Cian with a puzzled expression on my face. He shook his head and rolled his eyes. "These days your enemy wants to trash talk first before a battle. I blame Hollywood. I miss the days when you just went into battle. No pressure on having to match wits."

I nodded and stifled a chuckle. Ok I didn't stifle it but I tried.

The enraged vampires rushed us at once. I pulled upon all the magic I had and prayed to the Creator he would gift me with even more. I could feel Cian doing the same. Fomoire and Tuatha are cousins. We were created with the same strengths and skills though ours favored the land while the Fomoire favored the sea.

The vampires had speed but brought no weapons. They only had their fangs. Cian and I spread out a bit further, giving one another room. The first wave descended upon me. Not having to block swords I was surprised at how fast I was. I sliced through necks the second I had the opening. I didn't check on Cian, I knew he would be fine.

I wasn't having to move too much since the vampires were coming to me. I saw five rush past me towards Emrys and Neil. I knelt down and jumped as hard as I could doing a backflip landing in front of Neil and between the vampires. I took their heads and rushed back to the mass.

I heard Emrys, "Morrigan, I can't hold it much longer. Hurry!"

I was making progress as was Cian but we weren't half way through the vampires. There were still about fifty left.

"Cian!" I shouted. "Emrys doesn't have long. We need to join."

I didn't trust Cian and joining was rarely used. Once we did, we would be bound to each other's emotions for about a day and completely drained of energy. Essentially we would have to rest a full day, feeling what the other felt, in the land of the Godless. I knew it was a terrible idea but we couldn't take on two hundred more enemies, especially the wolves if the bubble failed.

Cian and I kept battling the vampires slowly making our way to one another until we were side by side.

"You ready?" He yelled.

I wasn't. He saw the hesitation. "You are worried you will fall in love with me aren't you Red?"

My stomach churned. He was extremely handsome and knew it. He was slimy like the black seaweed he came from.

"You're an ass! Let's do this." I said as I grabbed his hand.

We pulled our magic and bound it together. Our other hands had to momentarily drop our swords and aim it at the vampires. A deep boom, like the sound barrier being broken sounded and our power shot out in front of us. The gold and blue light we created in our joining radiated into each vampire turning them to ash.

We both fell to the ground. I held Cian's hand, mostly trying to hold onto my consciousness.

I felt Neil pick me up. I knew it was Neil by how I fit. I let my head fall against his chest. I soaked in his smell. I was awake still. But barely.

Emrys was holding the bubble walking towards us. Towards the Great Oak. Making the bubble smaller with each step, keeping us safe inside.

Emrys spoke, "Neil, get the stone out of Morrigan's pocket. You hold her, I'll hold your hand, and I'll carry Cian over my shoulder. We need to step through the Great Oak quickly. I'm about to lose the shield."

I saw Emrys throw Cian over his shoulder. The scent and warmth of Neil. Of being in his arms. Feeling that familiar comfort, I drifted off to sleep.

CHAPTER 21

NEIL GENTLY LAID Morrigan on the ground while Emrys
semi-threw Cian down. He looked around the vast open area.
They had emerged from a giant rock, about the size of a house.
Other than that there was nothing. The ground was grey, the sky
was grey, the land flat, void of life or water. The air was warm; it
felt heavy and smelled of stagnant dust.

Neal spoke first, "What's wrong with them? Are they okay?"

Emrys plopped down a few feet away, leaning up against
the rock. "They're fine. They joined their powers to take out the
remaining vampires. It drained them of their energy. They'll sleep
for about a day to rejuvenate, and be fine."

Neil sat down next to Emrys. "I had no idea she could fight
like that. Or even had that kind of magic. That was amazing."

Emrys chuckled. "There's a lot you don't know, Neil."

"Who is Cian?" Neil asked, full of questions.

Emrys closed his eyes, tilting his head back. "I'm not here to
catch you up on the past. I don't particularly like you that much."

Neil cut his eyes away. "We're stuck here for a day with nothing
to do. And I know you don't like me. I'm sure Morrigan hates me. I
couldn't help falling in love with Riley. It happened, *okay!*"

Emrys sat in silence for several minutes.

Neil said, "What if the Godless come while Morrigan and
Cian are out? What if—"

Emrys cleared his baritone voice, "Oh for crying out loud, you aren't going to shut up, are you? Pray the Creator that the Godless don't find us. We haven't a chance at the moment. I'm exhausted, our best warriors are asleep and you are too busy trying to chat. Here's the dummy's version for you. Cian's father was leader of the Fomoire. The Fomoire and Tuatha are cousins. Fomoire ruled the seas and Tuatha the land, ridding the realm of demons or any other evil creatures that would do the helpless humans harm. When Morrigan's father was a new King, he and Cian's father, who was King of the Fomoire, met to discuss an uprising. The humans, I'm sure at this point egged on by one of the Gods, had become fearful of the Tuatha and Fomoire. They believed that they would enslave them. There were Tuatha and Fomoire that had battled a great beast that had terrorized the island. Large sea creatures sinking boats. Massive half-animal half-human looking creatures killing the villagers. The Tuatha and Fomoire went and cleared the city of the demons. They had a great feast and celebration afterwards. The unsuspecting Tuatha and Fomoire were beheaded as the local king made a toast to them."

Neil interjected, "That's why you guys are suspicious of humans, isn't it?"

Emrys nodded. "Well that was the start of it, at least. Morrigan's father knew the humans were scared and being manipulated by the Gods. Cian's father didn't care why they did it, he wanted them destroyed."

"So what happened?" Neil was leaning forward at the tale.

Emrys raised one eyebrow. "You ever hear of Atlantis?"

"No way..." Neil's eyes bugged out.

Again, Emrys nodded. "Yes, that was the city of Atlantis. After Morrigan and Cian's fathers parted, the Fomoire descended upon the city and with their power, sunk it right into the ocean. By the way, all the places the humans have looked is not where it was, and there wouldn't be a trace. It was sunk all the way beneath the ocean floor. Wiped clean."

"That was the start of them becoming enemies?" Neil asked.

"Yes." Emrys looked saddened. "They are not meant to be enemies. The realm needs both of them. The Gods were either trying to destroy them at the same time or get them to destroy each other, and it has nearly worked."

Emrys caught Neil up on what Druantia had told them. Neil's shoulders slumped at the weight of it all.

"We can't fail at this, can we?" Neil's voice was small. It wasn't really a question.

Emrys put his hand on the young man's shoulder. "No, we cannot. I think the Creator has a plan, and I believe in my heart, even though the odds are drastically stacked against us, that we will prevail. We have the most powerful Fomoire warrior, the most powerful Tuatha warrior, and a King of Erin all working together to try to save the realm. But I have no doubt the cost will be high."

Neil sat for a while taking it in. "So what happened to Cian's father?"

Emrys shook his head. "That, I do not know. Since I was awakened I've never come across any Fomoire. Not a single one. I hadn't a clue they still existed until Cian walked in."

"Can we trust his help?" Neil asked.

Emrys' eyes narrowed. "Cian's father and brothers are the ones that killed Morrigan's family. Our King, our Queen, and her three brothers. Morrigan only survived because she had just left with me to go on a quest. They thought she would be there as well. She would have been killed too."

Neil sat in silence.

Emrys said, "King Conall was leader of the Teulu. He didn't make it to the family in time, but he killed Cian's brothers. Morrigan and Cian weren't there when this happened, but every time they've ever met in battle they try like hell to take the other one's head. So I guess you could say there is some bad blood between them."

Neil shook his head.

Emrys added, "And now they're stuck in one another's heads for a day. Who knows, maybe Morrigan will get some answers."

"Wait, what?" Neil perked up.

Emrys replied, "Joining is rarely done. If done improperly it can kill you. If you are lucky, like they were, you're able to stop before your life force drains from you and you're put into a deep sleep. Since they joined in essence, their life force, their magic, they share a bond and while sleeping they are inside one another's minds… so to speak. It's a dreamlike state. Whatever Cian dreams is what Morrigan is dreaming, and vice versa. Like most dreams, you cannot control them. You are a spectator."

"That sounds intrusive," Neil offered.

"Well of course it is, dummy," Emrys scoffed. "Now can I please get some rest? I'm drained myself, and once they awaken tomorrow we have a bunch of Godless we have to convince to give us a sword, some magic God killing weapons, and oh yeah, hope they don't eat us."

CHAPTER 24

MORRIGAN LAY ON a white sandy beach. The air was clean and salty as the sun warmed her even though the cool waves trickled over her toes. She sat up, looking at the cloudless blue sky and the bright turquoise ocean.

She knew she was in Cian's dream. She dreaded and wondered what Cian would see in hers. Being bound like this was frustrating. It didn't seem fair that you could never know what the other person was seeing about you. But life was rarely fair.

She looked behind her, but the details were blurry. The dream wanted her to look at the ocean. She stared at the water, appreciating the beauty and gentleness of it when she heard a child laughing. She turned to see a small boy, about five years old she guessed, giggling about fifty feet away on the beach. He was up to his ankles in the water, staring out at it. His long black hair blew behind him in the ocean breeze. Large blue eyes searched the water. Not scared, but in anticipation. A large man burst out of the water ten feet from him and he jumped. The man landed next to the boy and picked him up. The boy laughed hysterically, as only a child can.

Cian stood with the small boy now on his hip and said as he stared at the water, "Where do you think Mommy is?"

They walked up and down the beach for a few minutes and Cian sat the boy down. "I guess Mommy left us."

A woman jumped out of the water landing on the other side of the boy as he squealed and jumped into her arms. "Mommy! Mommy! I found you!"

"Yes you did, my little shrimp," she said, poking his bare belly. She had long black hair that shone dark blue in the sunlight. She was beautiful. Long and lean, very strong. Her heart shaped faced had chiseled cheeks and large blue eyes that matched the boy's.

"I didn't know Cian had a wife and son." Morrigan said, realizing she was talking to herself. "By the Creator, it's not like they can hear me." She screamed, "Hey asshole what the hell happened to make you such a douchebag?"

Cian, his wife, and son were playing in the sand. Not paying any attention to Morrigan's taunts.

Morrigan rolled her eyes at herself. The family played in the sand for hours, or maybe minutes. Hard to tell in dreams.

The whole scene went blurry and then she was in a room. A large rectangular trough at least twelve feet in length presided in the center of the room, a fire contained in it. The walls were of dark wood and bore tapestries depicting oceans around the world. The scents of cinnamon and oak wafted through the air. Cian, his six brothers and his father were drinking ale at a table next to the fire. They were laughing and talking. She could not make out their words, but they were enjoying one another's company. One would stand and reiterate something and hit Cian on the shoulder while the others laughed. Cian laughed as well, hanging his head low, shaking it. They were teasing him about something.

Cian, his brothers and father were at the table in the same room but the scene shifted. No laughter and mugs of ale this time. Their faces were tight and Cian stood and yelled, "This is madness! All of you! We do *not* serve the Gods. You know they cannot be trusted. They mislead and twist everything to serve themselves and nobody else. You *have* to see this. You must know this in your hearts! This will be our undoing!"

The Fomoire King stood and said, "You are being unreasonable and shortsighted, Cian."

Cian stormed out of the room and the room vanished.

Cian was running up the beach where he and his family had played earlier in the dream. He had on his black and blue fish scale leathers. His sword was out and his face was panicked. About forty Fomoire in battle gear followed him with the same panic on their faces.

He and the others reached a village nestled next to the ocean. The flames were gone but smoke still drifted into the sky. Buildings were mostly burned but some were still intact. The smell of blood and death filled the air. Bodies of burnt headless Fomoire littered the ground. Thousands of them. Cian rushed towards the main hall, stepping around bodies, and flung open the large oak double doors. Hope filled his chest, the building showed no signs of fire. His wife and son were not burned, but their severed heads lay next to their crumpled bodies. He dropped to his knees. The loss was overwhelming, his chest felt as if it split open and everything ripped out. His body shook and convulsed as tears streamed from his eyes. He could barely see, but as he lifted his gaze he saw his father sitting on the throne. His face bore a look of shock, a few feet away on the ground.

The scene shifted again. The forty or so Fomoire and Cian stood outside the village. They raised their hands and balls of fire arced up into the air, sending what was left into flames. They sat on the beach, numb, and watched the village and their loved ones burn. When nothing was left but ashes, they once again extended their arms out, intertwining their powers, sending the remains into the earth. Nothing was rebuilt where the village once was.

Morrigan felt herself back in her own mind and body. She was groggy but felt well. Sleep began to fall away and her eyes opened.

She blinked a few times and saw a smirking smile and bright blue eyes. "Man oh man, you are one kinky chick," Cian teased.

CHAPTER 25

WE WALKED IN silence. Well almost silence, Emrys had opened up a link between our minds and I relayed Cian's dreams.

Neil pulled us away from our conversation. "Are we sure we're headed in the right direction? We've been walking for what must be half a day and still there's nothing. I can see for miles and nothing. The damn sun doesn't even move in this place."

I expected Emrys to answer Neil, but Cian spoke up, "You really aren't that bright, are you? There are no Gods here. The sun stopped in the sky where it was when the Gods were killed. The realm is frozen in place."

Emrys couldn't help smiling as he said, "I'm sure we're going in the right direction. We've been traveling almost a full day, by the way. We might as well stop here and rest."

We sat and I stretched out my tight muscles. Cian had acted his normal smartass self but he hadn't looked me in the eye all day. I'm sure he, like me, wondered what I had seen in his dreams.

"Can I have a drink?" I asked Cian.

He closed his eyes, waved his hand over the tattoo of the cup, mumbling some words, and opened his palm. He handed me the Cup.

"This is the Cup of Plenty?" I said, observing the ornate knot work on it.

"The one and only." He winked

I lifted it to my lips and tipped my head back. Water flowed from it and I drank until I was quenched. I passed it to Emrys.

"And how did you say you came to be in possession of it?" I asked, smiling, knowing he wouldn't tell me.

He smirked. "Oh Red, your charms won't work on me."

He was a slimebag and maybe it was the empathy I felt for him, but I laughed.

Emrys decided to join in. "Come now, she has no charm." Then he kicked at my boot playfully.

I couldn't resist. "Apparently you're the one with all the charm. Why, I had no idea you've had a love affair going on for what? Centuries? You've been holding out on me," I teased, remembering him and Druantia.

He gave me a look, warning me not to reveal too much. I knew better than to do that, but I rarely had a card to play against him and it felt good for a change.

Emrys passed the Cup to Neil then stretched his arms above his head. "So Cian, now that we have a bit of time to kill why don't you fill us in on how you came to be friends with the Vampire King."

We all looked at Cian. He looked calm as ever and started, "See, so what happened was—"

"Stop," I said. "Cut the bull and tell the truth, or by the Creator I will end you this instant."

"Simmer down, Red." He smiled as he took the cup back from Neil and pushed it against his forearm, returning it to the tattoo. "Okay. Cards on the table, I suppose." He sighed and his face became serious. "Long story short, after you were put to sleep, Artaius turned on us. There was a team of us away on a quest. An unsanctioned quest actually. When we returned all of our people were dead. There are only thirty-seven Fomoire in existence now."

Emrys and I knew this to be true from the dream I had seen. But it didn't make sense so I asked, "Wait... now? If that was over a thousand years ago why haven't your numbers grown?

Cian shook his head. "We've never been able to reproduce since.

I don't have an explanation, other than the damn Gods, possibly. Anyway, we went into hiding. We feared a large number of us would attract the attention of the Gods and we wanted to stay hidden so we dispersed into groups of no more than four together at any time around the world. We only met once a year on Samhain."

Emrys and I nodded in understanding a great loss of your people. Neil acted as though he were listening to a fairy tale. He couldn't begin to know what it felt like.

Cian said, "For some reason or another, since the day of our battle there have been few demons. We led quiet lives, trying to gather information on Artaius. It was nearly impossible. Centuries went by. No demons to interrogate, no sign of any of the Gods or any other supernaturals. We began taking turns traveling to the different realms but found nothing. Oddly enough, I was walking home one night in Rome. This was probably five hundred or so years ago. I heard something behind me a human wouldn't be able to hear. I kept walking and a person jumped down from a building right in front of me. He landed on his feet, uninjured, and smiled. He had fangs."

"That was the first time you ever saw a vampire?" I asked.

"Yes. Turns out there were four of them behind me. The one in front was supposed to distract me as his buddies came up from behind to drain me. They like to play with their food first. It didn't work out for them, to say the least. That month Kate, another Fomoire, and I ran into a dozen more. Also came across six werewolves."

"They're hellhound-human hybrids, by the way," Emrys interjected.

"Yeah, I figured that out," Cian replied. "We got together with everyone that Samhain and the others had come across vampires and werewolves as well. The humans were even aware of them to an extent. Not many that had seen them lived to tell. A few had witnessed attacks though, and so the lore began.

We decided to begin meeting at a different location once a month. The others observed only, while Kate and I went to see the Ogre King. He has a seer—"

Emrys interrupted, "Yes. She's a real bitch, by the way."

"Well, she *is* an ogre." Cian shrugged. "She told me that she saw the realm being destroyed. That was the path. I would have to find a way to change the path. That was all she said. Not very helpful and nothing about vampires or werewolves."

He wiped his brow then continued, "We figured out that the vamps and wolves were highly organized."

Neil cut in, "Yes we know. Kings, a Prime—"

"Sure, act like you know what's going on, kid." Cian turned away ignoring Neil. "The Prime is Artaius. He created them."

"You're sure?" Emrys asked.

"Very sure. He cut some kind of deal with the demons in Hell and created the vamps and wolves. They're loyal because he's told them they're part of an army. That Hell is going to open up, and that when it does they are the ones that will have to fight the demons in order to save the realm. Then they can rule over the humans. I'm assuming he told the demons the same sort of thing. Playing both sides. Or maybe he said it so that they would let him use their blood in order to create his hybrids. Who knows?"

He paused for a moment. We said nothing.

"About a hundred years ago I heard of a Hoodoo priestess that lived deep in the Bayou. She must've been a descendant of a very strong Druid. She knew when she saw me what I was. She told me I had to awaken my enemies. She did some spell and put whatever she mixed up into a jar. Said to sprinkle it over the Earth where they slept and that one of 'her people' would rise up. He'd take care of the others."

"She had more than Druid in her. She's a seer of some kind. Even I cannot see the future," Emrys said.

Cian nodded in agreement. "Strange times we live in. I didn't question it. She told me that my path wasn't to cross with yours until the Creator needed it to. That you would have to go on your own journey before we intersected. She told me I would need to leave the 'story of the sword' for you and to leave a message that when the

Creator brought you to me, you would know I was a friend and not a foe. I was to get the Cup of Plenty and stone to the Godless and keep them on me at all times… then wait."

"Okay, so you woke Emrys up. How did you end up with the vampires? A vampire King no less," Neil said accusingly.

Cian didn't even look at him. "It took me almost eighty years to find and get the Cup of Plenty and the stone. It was not an easy task to say the least. Afterwards, I went to New York. I heard rumors in Europe that the vampire King of North America lived there. I've been there ever since. I finally found the king but kept my distance. This past year rumblings began about entire nests vanishing without a trace. I figured Emrys had finally found a way to awaken the Tuatha and you were the cause of the missing nests. I went there to tell the king I knew who and what was taking out his vampires and werewolves."

"You were selling us out?" Neil yelled.

Cian smiled widely. "Well it was hardly selling you out. Werewolves spotted a couple of redheads: one, a massive hulk of a man that I'm assuming is Daur, in New Orleans. Artaius knows it's Tuatha that are hunting his creatures by now, surely. I'm assuming the king was curious as to what I knew and how I knew of the Tuatha. I was meeting with him when it was announced you had arrived and I asked if I could greet you in order to verify my suspicions. Though I was trying to get my, 'I'm a friend' message out before you did anything, I obviously wasn't expecting you. I went there to get in front of the king and was hoping to get some information on how he contacts Artaius."

Cian wiped his forehead with his arm. His face became very stern. "I've waited a long time to track down Artaius. He took everything from me. I'm not opposed to saving the realm, but I will not rest until Artaius is dead."

Nobody had anything to say after that. We lay down and shut our eyes. We would be facing the Godless before much longer.

CHAPTER 26

NEIL

We walked endlessly through this damned land. Emrys led,
Cian and Morrigan next to one another, and me bringing up the
rear. I could feel the apprehension pressing into me. There was
no wind. The stagnant air not only held no life, it felt like it was
drawing life from me.

Morrigan refused to even glance my way. It pained me to have
her so cold towards me. The moment I laid eyes on her when she
returned I knew I had made a mistake with Riley. Hell, I knew
the first time I slept with Riley it was a mistake. Riley looked at
me as if I was strong and wise. Not just a man, but a King and a
hero. I always felt inferior to Morrigan. She was the one that was
strong and wise. I could never be her equal, much less someone
she could look up to or look to for help or guidance. I succumbed
to my ego with Riley. I cared for her but what drew me to her was
the way she made me feel about myself if, I was being honest.

Emrys kept his eyes trained on the horizon and said, "I see
the castle. About another five hours and we'll be there."

I shaded my eyes and squinted. "I don't see anything."

Emrys' voice was neutral for a change. "You wouldn't.
You're human."

How my life had changed. I walked as a King of Erin with
the leader of the Teulu of the Tuatha who was a queen, the most

powerful of the Fomoire and Emrys, Merlin himself. I was the inferior of them all and I knew it. I kept trying to prove myself worthy of my birthright. A descendent of King Arthur. I had felt myself get stronger and more skilled in my trainings over the past year. I easily bested every Knight. But I couldn't compete with the supernatural. I was only needed to get the sword of the Tuatha back. I would never have their respect. I would never have Morrigan's respect.

Seeing Morrigan fight beside Cian demoralized me even more. I was cheered and revered by my Knights for having led them into vampire nests and taking out dozens of them at a time. Morrigan took out hundreds effortlessly. She fought next to Cian in perfect synchronization. They were mesmerizing to watch. They were powerful, deadly and beautiful all at once.

I felt like a fool. All the times in training I 'bested' her. She let me win as a parent lets a child win.

Cian walked next to Morrigan and they discussed strategy for when we met the Godless. They spoke to one another as respected equals, even if neither of them trusted the other. Cian occasionally glanced back at me, giving his smug smile. He was an arrogant asshole.

Morrigan looked back at me and for a moment held my eyes. I missed her. The hardness in them returned but for a split second it was as it had been before she had left.

Emrys pulled me away from my thoughts as he said, "Cian what do you know of the Godless? Can they be reasoned with?"

Cian's voice even sounded like powerful crashing waves. "Well, if history holds true, this is a fool's errand and we'll all die and be eaten today."

I cringed at his steadiness and lack of fear. "But having the stone to enter the land and presenting the Cup of Plenty will garner us an audience with their King. I fear that we are going in blind as to whether they're reasonable or not. I'm hoping they will be intrigued by us wanting to save our realm from the Gods and be willing to help us out."

"Great, our plan is based on your hope," I scoffed.

Cian stopped and turned to me. "Hope is all we have right now. The entire realm, everyone we love, is counting on us and all is lost if we don't succeed. I have faith the Creator will present a solution once we arrive."

He turned away and walked on, as did the others. They seemed to be okay with hoping for a miracle. I would've much rather had a plan. We walked in silence as the castle of the Godless came into view.

CHAPTER 27

NEIL

The castle was in view a few hours before we reached it because it was a massive fortress. The grey stones rose out of the ground, in keeping with the monochromatic scheme of the land. It resembled an English castle I once saw in a movie. A moat that dried up long ago was now a deep trench. The gates were down and open. No guards were posted outside. This was not a place that was trying to keep anyone out. It was a place that welcomed any and all in, never to leave.

We walked across the bridge to the gates and into the courtyard. There was no one in sight. The far side of the courtyard had a set of stairs leading inside. The steps were each three feet high, the arched doorways at least fifty. I craned my neck to look up to the top tower. It rivaled any skyscraper in New York City.

Emrys led the way and we scaled the stairs to the main entrance. Every step closer increased the putrid smell that came from within.

"What is that stench?" I asked. "It smells like a hundred corpses that have been dug up after a year."

Nobody answered. Which meant that nobody knew.

We stepped inside the entrance and Emrys projected his voice, "We have an invitation stone and a gift. A Cup of Plenty to be presented in return for an audience with the King."

We looked at one another but nobody spoke. Seconds ticked by slowly but felt slower still. The putrid smell increased though we hadn't moved. The ground began to vibrate slightly. The door at the end of the hall opened and the Godless stepped through.

With the opening of the door the smell rushed down to hit us in the face. I could see everyone's eyes begin to water and noses wrinkle. My stomach lurched, fighting to keep my gag reflex from winning. The Godless were as massive as we expected, towering around thirty feet high. The one large bulbous eye planted in the center of their head is what I expected would shock me most. Seeing a real life Cyclops was startling enough, but the zombie like appearance had my nerves screaming at me to get out of there.

Tendrils of flesh hung from their head where hair should be. Their skin and eyes were the same grey hue of the landscape. Their sunken bellies and protruding ribs increased their grotesqueness. A simple piece of cloth was tied around their waists but their testicles hung below, swaying as they walked. Their skin hung from them like limp dried crepe paper.

Cian whispered, "This is what happens without the Gods."

I couldn't tell if he was stating or asking.

Four guards arrived with spears pointed at us. The head guard said, "Let me see the stone and the cup."

Cian removed the cup from its tattoo on his arm and held it up as Morrigan held up the stone. The guard reached for the cup and Cian quickly returned it to his arm.

He bowed and said, "My apologies, I am prepared to present the cup to the King and only the King."

The guard grumbled something to the others, the single eye looking like it would pop under the pressure of the scowl on his face.

The guard said, "Follow me."

We walked with two guards in front of us and the other two behind us. I wished for supernatural powers against such beasts. If we had to fight our way out, Morrigan, Cian and even Emrys were equipped to do so. They would protect me since I was needed, but I wouldn't be able to protect myself.

We wound through the halls deep into the belly of the castle until we entered into the throne room. The walls rose at least a hundred feet into the air. Dozens of Godless were assembled there. Male and female, all looking as emaciated as the guards. There were no tables or chairs, tapestries or adornments. The King sat on a throne at the end of the room with his legs wide, elbows on his knees. He saw us and indulged in a long scratch of his testicles as we approached.

The guards had us stop about ten feet from the King, and we took a knee out of respect. The head guard went to him and whispered in his ear. He looked no better off than the others. Though they didn't look feeble, they looked very aged and lifeless.

The King said, "So you have an invitation stone and a Cup of Plenty. You have an audience with me. I am King Harris. Speak."

Cian stood, removed the Cup from his forearm once again, took the stone from Morrigan and approached the King. He knelt and held his hands out as he spoke. "King Harris, we are of the Earthly realm. I am Cian, King of the Fomoire. I travel with Morrigan, Queen of the Tuatha, the great Druid Lord Emrys, and the true King of Erin, Neil. Long ago, one of the Druids sent the sword of the Tuatha, originally forged here and gifted to one of Morrigan's descendants, back here in order to protect it from falling in the hands of evil. It is bonded to Neil, King of Erin, and we have come to retrieve it. We bring a Cup of Plenty so that you and your people will never thirst again, as a gift to show respect to you and your people."

The King's bulbous eye bounced around each of us. It's hard to read someone when they only have one eye, and I couldn't tell how this was going.

The King motioned to one of the guards who took the stone and cup from Cian and gave it to the King.

He took the cup and held it to his lips. Slowly, he tipped his head back. The cup was working; he drank for a long time and then passed it to another. The murmurs grew and the Godless began pushing one another to get to the cup.

"Enough!" the King bellowed.

The crowd stilled.

He continued, "You will all get a turn, my people. This is a great day."

The Godless cheered. We smiled. This was turning out well.

He smiled and said, "It's been centuries since I've drunk my fill. I cannot thank you enough. The few dozen of us that you see are all that is left of us. We do not die of starvation or thirst, because there is no God to take our lives. The only way we experience death is if killed, and we cease to exist since there is no God to take us to the afterlife. Most of my people have gone mad and begged for loved ones to kill them so they didn't have to endure this anymore."

"Great King Harris," Cian began. "We hope that the gift is pleasing enough that you would return the Great Sword of the Tuatha to Neil?"

The King nodded and made a gesture with his hand to one of the guards. The Godless continued to pass the cup around.

A few minutes later the guard appeared with the sword. I was drawn to it. The closer the guard brought it the more anticipation filled me. He handed the hilt of it to me and I took it. The sword glowed momentarily and I felt a rush of power pulse through me.

"He's definitely the one bonded to the sword. Consider it returned and your gift accepted." King Harris nodded to me.

"We have one more thing to ask of you, Great King," Emrys spoke now. "The Gods of our world are trying to unleash a realm of demons in order to destroy us. We are trying to stop them from doing this and the sword of the Tuatha is the only enchanted one in our realm. The only thing we have to protect ourselves from the Gods and the demons as well if they are released. We know it is an imposition but we are humbled to ask if you would grace us with more weapons so that our realm is not destroyed."

The King once again returned to scratching his testicles. They bobbed around as he pondered then said, "What do you present as gift for this favor?"

Emrys spread his arms and answered, "We traveled in great haste, and did not have time to bring a gift for this request. But the Tuatha have a cauldron that never empties and never leaves anyone hungry, much like the Cup of Plenty. We could return with it?"

I looked at Morrigan since the cauldron was of the Tuatha. If she didn't know of the plan she showed no surprise. She wore that damn blank face that she put on when she didn't want anyone to know what she was thinking.

The Cup of Plenty was passed back to the King and he took another long drink from it. Once he cleared his throat he began, "I am no fool. You want me to give you weapons that would kill Gods in return for a cauldron that you may or may not bring back. We have starved here for centuries, only eating the few who are stupid enough to try to get those weapons. We can't leave our realm because the Gods of other realms would surely hunt us down and torture us more than we are tortured now. If your realm loses its Gods, then that would leave us free to go there and eat whatever animals and vegetation are left."

"We didn't think this plan through thoroughly, did we," Cian mumbled.

"Clearly," Morrigan. replied

The King said, "I presented the sword to the King of Erin. He is the one bonded to it. And out of respect for the time when it was forged and gifted, I will allow him to return to your realm."

King Harris tossed me the stone we used to enter from New York.

He turned to look at the others. "He, and he alone, may leave. You three will stay and be our feast and celebration."

"No!" I yelled.

One of the guards used his spear to knock me to my knees. Morrigan rushed to my side and helped me up.

Her eyes looked softly at me. Pleading with me. She said urgently, "Neil, you must go. You must take the sword and find Conall. Please."

I cupped her face in my hands. "I can't leave you. I won't leave you. I won't do it."

Morrigan gently removed my hands form her face and handed me the sword. "Neil, trust in me. Trust in me. Take the sword and get back to that giant rock as fast as you can. The stone will allow you to enter it. Focus on our Great Oak. Think of nothing else. This rock will work, even though you're human. It will get you back. You must survive this. You must get the sword back."

I felt like a helpless coward. I slowly stepped backwards, looking at Morrigan. Her face was relieved. I looked at Emrys and Cian expecting mocking expressions, accusing me of cowardice, but they looked relieved as well. I knew they planned to survive somehow but as skilled as they were, the Godless were massive. They were going to sacrifice themselves so that I could return the sword to Conall. They would die here and I would live. My only purpose, not to be the leader or hero—just dumb luck being born with the right blood in my veins to carry a sword back to its real owner.

CHAPTER 28

MORRIGAN

The tightness in my chest loosened at seeing Neil safely turn the corner. He was free. He would get the sword back to Conall. Half of this quest was accomplished.

The Godless King turned to us and smiled wickedly. "Put them in the cages. We will be feasting tonight!"

The other Godless cheered and we were picked up and carried further into the castle to a dungeon.

The guard enjoyed throwing us into the cell, but I was glad that we weren't separated.

"Well we safely got the sword of the Tuatha out of here and on its way home. Now all we have to do is escape, find the weapons, and a way back to our realm," I said with more cheer in my voice than normal.

"So, this is what you would consider a good day?" Cian said, smiling, leaning against the wall.

My spirits were light. I replied, "I didn't think they would let Neil just go. And look… they didn't take our weapons." I smiled, wiggling my swords.

Emrys chimed in as gloomily as ever, "That's because they plan on using those as toothpicks to pick our bones out of their teeth."

Cian ignored the comment. "Emrys, can you blast them and

freeze the King so we can question him as to where the weapons are then get back home?"

Emrys stared at Cian blankly before replying, "Blast them? Really Cian? It's a lot more complicated than that!"

I could feel Emrys' temper bubbling. "I assume by *blasting* them you mean can I create fire from thin air and hit them with pinpoint accuracy? Is that what you mean?"

Cian didn't pay any attention to Emrys' tantrum. "Yes, that's exactly what I mean. Blasting." He smiled playfully.

Emrys threw his hands up in the air and sat down. Wearily he replied, "Magic is not... magic. Things do not just happen. I cannot create anything. What I do is more like transfer, or manipulate elements. I can tap into the life, the energy, around me and use that to do my bidding. There is no life here. Even the Godless themselves are almost lifeless. You saw them. They're like husks, shells of what they were. Their souls are not even enough to power a small flame to light a cigarette."

Emrys shook his head helplessly. "I can draw upon my own essence but not enough to take them all out."

Cian nodded. "Can you draw upon us?" He looked at me as he spoke.

Emrys shook his head. "I'm not willing to do that."

I started to interject but Cian interrupted me. "Let me rephrase then. Can you draw upon me?"

Emrys sat still. Without looking up he made the smallest of gestures. A nod.

Cian slapped Emrys' back and sounded jolly. "Well it's a good thing you're going to draw upon me rather than Morrigan. I'm more powerful anyway, and have the strength to spare." Then winked at me.

I couldn't help but burst into laughter. "You're an ass." But there was no bite to my words.

"I will do my best to not drain you, Cian," Emrys said. I could tell he was developing a plan.

I turned and put my hands on each side of my old friend's face. "You will draw upon me if you have to. I won't take no for an answer."

Before Emrys could say any more, one of the Godless came back and began unlocking our cell.

The door to our cell was small to him. He squeezed his hand in to grab me. I took the opportunity and drew my swords, driving them into the center of his palm. Before he could retract I twisted them, thrusting upwards so his palm was face up. Cian put his hands on mine and helped me drive straight down, pinning his hand. The Godless screamed and used his other hand to try to pry it free. Cian and I used all of our combined strength to hold him. Emrys quickly grabbed the long sword strapped to Cian's back and sliced open the wrist of the Godless.

Blood that looked like honey began to flow. With each pump of his panicked heart, more blood oozed into the room. The entire floor was covered in it. It was thick and oily. I picked my boot up and could feel it stick a little.

The Godless still fought to free his hand but he was weakening.

Emrys stood at the edge of the bars. The large eyeball's lid began to flutter and droop. Emrys turned and placed a hand on the wrist of the Godless and spoke. I felt the magic thick in the air. Worry gripped me over how much it would cost Emrys. "Where do we find the weapons? The ones that will kill the Gods."

The weak Godless couldn't resist the compulsion. "You have it at this very moment. It is not magical weapons that we have. It is our blood. A weapon, any weapon, dipped in our blood will kill a God."

We stood in shock and looked at one another.

Cian broke the silence. "Explains why they aren't keen on sharing their weapons."

I nodded. They were grotesque creatures, but I couldn't help but pity them. I was sad for them. An entire thriving realm almost destroyed. Down to only a few dozen that we planned to wipe out and now drain them of their blood in order to save our own realm. Guilt gripped my chest. I thought of my children. Of my people. I hated this.

Cian sensed my feelings. I'm not sure if it was a remnant of our bonding or if he could just relate since both of us had experienced near extinction of our people.

He still held his hands over mine, helping me hold the swords down. His hands softened since the Godless had no more fight in him and he said, barely above a whisper, "We haven't a choice but it doesn't make this any easier. We do the dirty work. We would be monsters if we didn't feel the weight of it."

I didn't trust him. Not for a second. I knew in every fiber of myself that he was helping us for his own agenda. But I also knew he meant what he said and he was one of the few people that truly understood the burden I felt.

The Godless went limp as the life bled out of him. I pulled the swords out and we pushed his arm back through the door.

Time to do this.

"Emrys, how are you doing? You good?" I dipped my swords in the blood that covered the floor of the cell and appraised him as best I could. He was still a mystery to me, and even I had trouble reading him at times.

"Right as rain, love," he said, more lightheartedly than I was comfortable with. I knew he was hiding how weak he felt.

I kept my mask so I didn't betray my thoughts.

Cian must have had the same concern. He began dipping his weapons in the blood as well. "Morrigan, how about you and I work on taking these guys out? Emrys, let's hold you back as a reserve and only use your power if one of us is in dire trouble."

Emrys nodded in agreement. That couldn't be good. He would never agree to this if he were at full strength.

Emrys led the way out of our cell. Cian and I exchanged a knowing glance. It was up to us.

We made our way without any trouble back to the throne

room. Peeking around the corner, we saw the remainder of the Godless standing around, anticipating the guard's return. To feast upon us.

"Now, how are the three of us supposed to feed that many?" Cian said, trying to lighten the mood.

Ignoring him I tilted my head towards the crowd. "Okay, let's go."

Cian grabbed my elbow, turning me to him. "Shouldn't we have a plan?"

Emrys stifled a chuckle. Cian looked at him, puzzled. Emrys held up one hand while holding his belly with the other silently laughing. "I forget you've always been on the other side of things. A plan?" Emrys chuckled a few more times. "That's a good one. You really are funny, Cian."

Cian looked at me, confused. I replied to his unasked question. "Yes, we have a plan. We go in there and kill them."

I took off before Cian could point out the flaw in my plan. That it wasn't a plan at all. The one thing I had learned was that there were times when you could plan an attack and that other times you had to just fight like hell to live and hope the Creator would grace you with victory.

As I ran, the fury that I'd been holding in began to build and come to the surface. This wasn't anger. I wanted to unleash the wrath that I felt. The pain of losing my people. The pain of Neil's betrayal. The pain at knowing that if we failed my realm would be destroyed. The pain that knowing the Gods had been plotting for centuries. The pain at having to wipe out the last of a race of beings. All of it, I let that ferociousness build in me and focused it.

The first Godless didn't know what hit him. I slashed through his Achilles and as he dropped to one knee I slit his testicles and ripped open his femoral artery. Before he could fall on me I climbed up his back and drove my swords into the carotid artery of the Godless next to him. A woman. She yelled as I held onto my sword with all my body weight as it slid through her skin, ripping it.

I jumped down as she fell and had to do a backflip out of the way of another Godless that was falling. Apparently Cian had joined the fight and had three down already.

"I'm winning! Three to two!" he yelled as he used the Achilles/testicle/femoral attack that I just had. "Make that four to two!"

"Prick!" I grimaced as I screamed it. Wow Morrigan, *that* was witty.

The Godless had shaken off their surprise and were now on the offensive. I jumped up at the nearest one and drove my sword deep into his chest. Before I could do more damage, his hand came up to grab at me so I pushed off and onto the next one. I landed on the shoulder of one of the guards. I plunged my long sword deep into his eye. Two of his friends were steps away. I turned and threw both of my medium swords and hit both of their eyes as well. I pulled my long sword out and as the other two fell to the ground I went to retrieve my medium swords.

As I was pulling the second one out a Godless kicked me and I flew into the wall. I fell to the ground hard enough to rattle me. I stood as he raised his spear—then he froze.

Cian emerged on his shoulder, having driven his sword into the base of the giant's skull.

The ass winked. "You're welcome, Red!"

I rolled my eyes and got back into the fight. I took down two more, getting back into my stride.

I looked to see Cian struggling to fight off three that had him cornered. I ran with all my speed and slashed them all through the Achilles. As they fell Cian stabbed their eyes.

"Those count as mine, and I should get double points for saving your sorry ass," I said as I headed back to the fight. I could feel his smile even though I never looked back.

I couldn't help myself but add, "And you're welcome!"

Cian fell in next to me and we continued fighting. We slashed our way to the throne where the King sat watching, as if it were a show. A guard stood on each side of him, the carnage of their people not affecting them in any way.

Emrys was beside me as we advanced towards the King.

The King stood and laughed. "No worries, boys. Now we each get a whole one to eat. A great feast indeed!"

The guards snorted and grunted laughter. There was no joy in their voices. If there was a sound to define wicked that was it.

The King said, "I am not weak like the rest of these fools. I am not King for nothing!"

Emrys, always the inquisitive one, couldn't help himself. "You have to answer me one question before this ends. We learned that it's the blood of your people that enchants weapons dipped in them to kill the Gods. How did that come to be?"

The King looked baffled that this man was asking such a question when he was surely going to face death. He obviously didn't know Emrys. Even if Emrys believed that he really was going to die, he'd still rattle off at least twenty questions.

The King's bulbous eye squinted at him. "What the hell. You will die anyway. Long ago one of our Goddesses fell in love with me."

The look of disgust on Cian's face distracted the King. "What? I'm very handsome and charismatic."

Cian shook his head. The King went on. "She had told me about the unrest of the Gods. She warned me that something was going on and that someone with great magic from another realm could help. A witch was brought here and she promised she could create a weapon that would kill a God, but it would come at a price. I didn't ask the cost. We needed something to protect ourselves. She performed a ritual and that was that. It's our blood. Not just a little blood either. Although it only takes a little of our blood to coat a weapon and it only needs to be coated once for it to always be a God killer, it has to come from one of us that was completely drained."

The King was mad from centuries of famine, thirst, and the demise of his people. He was wicked and cruel, no doubt. But in that moment the madness had lifted and I saw only his pain.

The King shook off the lucidity and trained his eye on me. He raised his hands above his head and a massive ball of white fire began to grow.

He growled, "I told you I was not King for nothing!"

The ball had grown to at least twenty feet in diameter and it shot straight for us faster than we would be able to move. We would not make it.

Emrys threw up a shield and dissipated the fire. The instant it burned out he unleashed a wave of the same white fire back at the King and the guards. The King had no shield. The fireball hit them squarely. Their gargled screams only lasted an instant. They fell and smoldered, and the fire burned out as their lives did.

Emrys fell to the ground.

I was on him immediately. "Emrys, take some of my energy. Take it, damn it. You need it."

He placed his weak hand on my shoulder. "Bitch, I'm planning on it," he said wearily with a half-hearted laugh.

I teared up laughing. I always felt better when he was being his sassy self. I felt the pull and drain on my power.

Emrys sat up, still very weak.

"You didn't take enough," I urged, embracing him.

"I took enough to stay alive. We're the only living creatures in this realm. As long as I don't have to *blast*," he paused, rolling his eyes playfully at Cian, "anyone anytime soon. I just need to rest. I'll be fine."

Cian kneeled down next to us. "Everyone is dead. There is no more threat. By now Neil has taken the sword safely back. Emrys, you rest as long as you need. Morrigan and I will try to find something to put the blood of the Godless in."

Emrys shook his head. "We need as much as we can get, and

how are we going to travel a full day, even when I've regained my strength, with all of it? No, that won't work."

Cian tilted his head. "Then what? You want to not take it?"

Emrys shook his head in protest. "No, not what I meant. I have an idea. Morrigan, you're not going to like it, but it's the only viable option."

I held my breath but said nothing, so he could continue.

"Cian, I am too weak at the moment, but if you let me draw on your power I can reverse the Cup of Plenty. Instead of pouring an unending supply of water from it, we can put all the blood we want into it. So it's an unending container of sorts."

Emrys was right. I didn't like the thought of him doing something that would drain him even more. I knew he would take little of Cian's power and use most of his own. Fear bubbled up into my throat.

Cian pulled the Cup of Plenty from the tattoo on his arm. "Use as much of my power as you need. We need every drop of their blood we can gather."

I sat there feeling helpless, staring at them. They held hands, looking at one another. It took me a moment to realize what was happening. Emrys had asked Cian to let him speak into his mind and Cian had agreed. They were having a conversation that I couldn't hear. The only reason Emrys wouldn't want me to hear it was because he thought this was dangerous.

"No!" I screamed.

I hadn't stopped screaming before it began. Both of their eyes had turned white. The cup rose into the air, a golden glowing halo radiating from it. Blood from the room began to form spiraling spinning droplets in the air. The blood that was on the floor, the blood that was still in their bodies, the blood that was in our cell streamed into the room. The spiral spun faster and faster until it looked like a giant tornado overhead. I looked away from it at Emrys and Cian. They hadn't moved. The bottom point of the blood tornado spun until it hovered above the Cup and as the white disappeared from both Emrys and Cian's eyes the blood drained into the Cup.

It fell to the ground with a clang as the two men's bodies slumped over. I was on Emrys in an instant. He was breathing, thank the Creator. I could hear his heartbeat. It was weak. I cried and tried to push my magic into him, but I only have a little magic compared to the great Druid. I only prayed it helped. His heart began to beat more strongly. I could hear it. It wasn't much, but it would have to suffice.

Cian began to mumble incoherently.

I went to him and knelt down. "Cian? Can you hear me? Are you okay?"

He was barely audible, even to me. "Just need rest."

Then he passed back out. They were both alive, but on the brink of being lost. I had no idea if either of them would make it. I dragged both of them to a corner of the room and then grabbed the Cup. I sat with my back against the wall and both of their heads on my lap.

Then I prayed and waited.

CHAPTER 29

I AWOKE WITH a start like I had been slapped. I opened my eyes quickly, looking around on full alert. I scanned the room. Nothing moved. Nothing had changed. A few dozen decaying Godless bodies littered the ground. It was the smell. They were putrid alive and rancid in death.

I shook my head, trying to clear it. I looked down and Emrys and Cian's heads still lay on my lap. I checked their pulses. Both were strong.

I let out a breath that felt as though I'd been holding it a lifetime. Relief poured over me. They were resting and out of the reach of death.

I gently ran my fingers through Emrys' silken hair. His face was peaceful and I hoped he was having dreams of happier times while he healed.

I stared down at Cian. How many times had we fought, trying to kill one another? How strange it was to have him here now. I could slit his throat and be done with him forever. I didn't need him anymore. Though I knew he was holding something back, I also knew he was not my enemy. Not at the moment, at least. I'd seen him as a devoted husband, loving father, caring son and brother. I hoped that he would not betray me and force me to kill him.

As if he could hear my thoughts he stirred and his eyes

opened. "Are you planning on slitting my throat in my sleep or are you going to lean down and gently kiss me?"

"I'm leaning towards the throat slitting if those are my only options," I said as I pushed his head off my lap and let it hit hard on the stone.

He rolled to his side and rubbed his head as he sat up. "Too soon for jokes? Woman, I was just on the brink of death." He gave me an exaggerated look of distress and said, "And all of this after I saved you from certain death."

"I believe I returned the favor," I replied.

He rubbed at his throat. "Right now I'm wishing we had not reversed the use of the Cup of Plenty. I'm dying of thirst. How long was I out? And for the love of the Creator what is that smell?"

I nodded towards the pile of bodies. "This damn place. With no setting or rising sun I'm not sure how long we were out. I poured what power I had left into Emrys and passed out not long after that. I have no idea how long it was for, but judging by the decay of the bodies it's been a while. But then again, I don't know how this realm works. I've not been awake long."

"So we wait for Emrys to wake up and then head back?" Cian said, standing, stretching his body out.

I gently sat Emrys' head down so that I could stand. My joints had stiffened as well. "That's the plan."

Cian lifted one side of his mouth into a smile. "Oh, so *now* you're keen on having a plan."

He could be irritating and arrogant but I had to admit I enjoyed his wit at times. I couldn't help but laugh. "Yes, I suppose once in a while I'm good with a plan. But only on special occasions."

Cian laughed this time. "Why Red, I had no idea you actually had a sense of humor."

"Daur finds me rather hilarious, actually," I said, beginning my training moves to further work out my muscles.

Cian fell into the same rhythm and joined me. "Daur probably finds farts funny."

My smile betrayed me. Cian stopped to look at me as he said, "See! I'm right!"

I continued going through the movements. "Yes, yes you're right. Still doesn't mean I'm not funny."

I felt a storm of emotion wash over me and said, "Wait until we get back. Now that I have the blood of the Godless on my sword, I'll be damn-right hilarious when I take Artaius' head."

Cian grunted an affirmation but said nothing.

Hours passed and Emrys still hadn't awakened. Cian helped me carry him to the entrance of the palace, away from the stench of the dead Godless.

He sat on the steps, letting his legs dangle. I sat down next to him. Far enough away so that he didn't get any ideas.

We stared out into the vastness. The sun hung unmoving in the sky. The lack of sound made my skin crawl. No breeze to rustle through the leaves. No animals scurrying around on the ground. Not even an insect to climb a blade of grass.

"Is this what will happen to our world if we go to war with the Gods?" he said, not bothering to look at me.

I scooted closer and put my hand on his shoulder. "Cian, we've fought for as long as I can remember. The Tuatha and the Fomoire. If we continue fighting this is exactly what will become of our world. We need to defeat Artaius and keep the Gods in our realm. We may need to kill some of them, but not all of them. There are many that are benevolent and couldn't care less about us or the humans, but as long as we can keep the realm functioning we have a chance. I'd love nothing more than to take the heads from each and every one of them."

I removed my hand from his shoulder and rested it in my lap, still watching the horizon that seemed never to end.

Cian stood and extended a hand to help me up. I let him.

He said sternly, "Morrigan, we will not let this happen in

our realm. I swear to you on my life, and all the lives lost to my people, we will work together to prevent this."

His voice dropped an octave and sounded guttural as he vowed, "But Artaius will die. He will pay for taking my wife, my child... my family."

"I pledge my sword and all my skill to help make that happen," I replied.

We both turned at the sound of footsteps.

Emrys was standing, reaching his massive arms far above his head. "How long was I out?"

I pointed to the sun. "Well when you passed out the sun was there. And when I awoke it was there. Oh and let's see now it's there. So my guess is, not even the gods know."

Emrys walked up to me and kissed me on the forehead. "You are rather hangry so apparently it's been a while."

"I'm hungry but not hangry," I said, bumping my hip into him.

He turned to speak to Cian as if I weren't there. "She gets very hangry when you don't keep her belly topped off. Always carry a protein bar or something with you because if she doesn't eat she's completely unbearable."

They laughed at my expense. I let them as I rolled my eyes.

"Okay, Emrys is awake. We have quite a walk ahead of us. Any idea how we're going to get through the big rock back to our realm?" I asked.

Emrys of course had an answer. "Easy," he said handing us each a stone. "The necklaces that the Godless wore had traveling stones on them. I took them while you were busy fighting."

"This is why I make you come with me," I said, giving him a big kiss and wrapping my arms around him.

Emrys had the cup in his hand. "Let's get this back home."

CHAPTER 30

THE WALK BACK to the rock seemed much longer. The hunger and thirst were making it a much slower trip. Emrys definitely wasn't back to one hundred percent—not that Cian and I were—and he struggled with each step.

Finally the giant rock came into view.

Emrys stopped to speak. "We each have a traveling rock. If ever in the future we need to meet in a safe place we meet here. Keep it around your neck at all times."

Cian and I nodded. Emrys had a way of always being prepared and thinking ahead. I wondered if it was because he knew what was coming or if it was just experience. Probably both but the foreboding look on his face gave me an uneasy feeling.

We each passed through the rock and came out through the Great Oak into Missouri. Our new home, as it were. I closed my eyes and lifted my face to the sky. It was night. No sun hanging frozen in the sky. The breeze brushed over my face. After having been in a void for so long the sounds that surrounded us seemed almost overwhelming.

Emrys put his hand on my shoulder. "Feels good to be back, doesn't it."

"I'm starving and thirsty, but I've never felt so happy," I said sincerely.

We had a long walk back to our home but our pace

quickened, the life around us fueling our souls. Emrys seemed to be soaking it in with each step. His chest rose higher, his shoulders straightened. My heart felt good seeing him strong again.

The large estate came into view. Lights illuminated the windows and judging from the moon's position it was still before midnight. Judging by the moon… I loved this realm.

We made our way quickly, even jogging until we came up the stairs to the massive oak double doors. I pushed them open and we entered the hall. None of us spoke but the other two followed me straight to the kitchen.

When we got there I tossed them each two bottles of water and grabbed a couple for myself. We sat at the marble island chugging our water then began to reach into the Cauldron, pulling out everything we could think of.

The island was covered in smoked venison, braised beef, roasted potatoes and carrots as well as salmon and kelp, the latter obviously being Cian's choice. We didn't use plates or silverware. There were no manners to be seen.

Daur entered the kitchen. "Holy gods, welcome back," he said, pulling up a stool and helping himself to the feast we had laid out. He didn't bother with utensils either, but that was nothing new.

Finally, our thirst quenched and bellies full, we began to slow.

Daur continued to stuff his face and in between bites said, "So when did you get back? And why aren't you in the big meeting with the King and everybody right now?"

He swallowed and added, "Can you believe everything that's happened in the past two days?"

We looked at each other and rose without a word. We used the speed that only a supernatural had and raced to the King's Library.

I burst through the doors first and stood center. Cian and Emrys flanked me.

We stood frozen for a moment, taking in the room. The large round table was occupied. Conall and Brian sat facing us. There were a few others I didn't recognize. Neil sat with his back to us, his surprised face looking over his shoulder. The one that had us momentarily paralyzed was the figure that sat to Neil's left. Artaius.

Suddenly, gathering our wits as if on cue, Emrys shot a white fireball at him as Cian and I threw our Godless soaked knives directly towards Artaius' head. The scene unfolded in slow motion. Neil jumped out of his chair and in midair turned into the largest werewolf I'd ever seen, landing right in front of Artaius. Protecting him. The fireball and our knives headed straight for the giant wolf's head. He never moved. Never flinched. He braced, making himself even bigger, to ensure he would be the target and not Artaius. Within inches of Neil, or the wolf… hellhound… or whatever he was, the knives dropped to the ground and the fireballs burned into nothing.

Artaius stood and slowly began clapping his hands. I still stared at Neil in his hellhound form. Yes, hellhound, that was it. His red lifeless eyes stared at me. Teeth bared, with black ooze slowly dripping from them. The matted hair on the back of his neck and back stood at attention. I couldn't take my eyes off of him, though I know I heard Conall speaking.

I felt Daur come up behind me. He chewed on a turkey leg—though more meat was caught in his beard than went into his mouth—as he said, "Told ya. Fucked up." Then he turned and continued down the hall.

"Conall!" I screamed in anger as I tried to move, but my feet were stuck.

I looked at Emrys and Cian and they were apparently experiencing the same problem.

"Just a precaution, dear Queen," Artaius said smugly.

Conall's face was furious and I saw him draw his sword. *His* sword. He had the sword of the Tuatha extended out to Artaius.

Artaius put his hands in the air nonchalantly, but his face showed no concern. "Easy now, good King." He turned to the others at the table. "Why don't we let King Conall get his Queen and her cohorts brought up to speed." He turned to Conall and bowed. "We'll resume this meeting another time."

He smiled at me. The same wicked smile that the Godless King had. Lacking any kindness, integrity or good. He snapped his fingers. Neil and the others disappeared into thin air.

My feet were released from the ground and I stormed up to Conall. Myself, Cian and Emrys were on him in an instant. All screaming at the same time.

Conall put his sword back in his sheath and sat down, rubbing his hands over his face. Something he did when his patience was about to run out. I didn't let that stop the barrage of insults I was slinging at him. Neither did the others. Brian took that as a sign to slip out of the room, shutting the door behind him.

Conall slapped the table and roared, "Enough!"

We stood in silence and Conall extended his arms. "Sit."

He looked at Cian. "Cian, it's been a long time since we've seen one another. I take it since Morrigan doesn't have your head on a spike, that you are a friend?"

Cian had his sarcastic arrogant act back on point. "I thought I was, but seeing as how you are good buds with the God that killed my family and nearly wiped out my people, I'm going to have to reconsider this friendship."

Conall nodded.

Before he could speak I interjected, "Artaius? And what is Neil doing as a hellhound? How long were we gone?"

He put his hands up before Emrys could begin an unending list of questions.

"Let me explain," he said. He looked weary. "You have been gone but four days. Obviously a lot has happened. Neil came back and returned the sword to me. He told me you were detained and didn't think you would make it back alive. I wasn't concerned, I knew better than that," he said, giving me his smile of surrender. "Brian and I continued with trainings and intelligence gathering. Neil came to see me to plead that there had to be another way other than going to war with the Gods. Having seen the land of the Godless and what their realm looked like, a victory over the Gods would not be a victory at all if that was what we were left with."

"It was rather dreadful," I confirmed.

"Yes, of course it is." Conall moved on. "That's why my plan was to only wipe out Artaius and his most trusted Gods, preventing the opening of the Hell realm, and then continuing on our merry way until the realms line up again in a few thousand years and they try a stunt like this again."

"Sounds smart enough," Cian said, nodding.

"Yes, yes. It was a decent plan," Conall said. "Except, I guess since I didn't feel compelled to share my plan with the wise old great King of Erin, douchebag Neil himself, he decided to handle things on his own. Because I'm a moron King who only has hundreds of years of experience ruling and defeating evil."

Conall's anger threatened to surface but he got it under control. "Neil summoned Artaius…"

Emrys interrupted. "How was Neil able to summon Artaius?"

Conall shook his head. "Let me back up. Neil's girlfriend Riley, the little Druid you left in charge, summoned Artaius for him."

"What?" Emrys screamed. "Why that little ignorant dumb—"

I patted Emrys' back. "They make quite the pair."

Conall stared at the two of us impatiently, waiting for us shut up. So we did.

"As I was saying," he said, looking at me. "Neil had Riley summon Artaius. Apparently Neil decided that he and his Knights were ill equipped to fight supernaturals. So Artaius offered the whole, 'how about I turn you into hellhounds and you answer to me and we'll fight together to keep Hell from being opened' option."

"Wait, what?" Cian said, shaking his head. "So Artaius is *not* trying to open hell? He's lying!"

Conall shrugged. "I don't know. When you walked in, I was meeting with Artaius, Neil as leader of the hellhounds, the new vampire King…"

He paused to look at me. "And yes, I said new vampire King because apparently you killed the previous one, which has unnerved Artaius."

I smiled. "Good. Mission accomplished."

Conall couldn't help but smile. "I was none too upset to hear that. So anyway, we were meeting because Artaius wanted to offer a truce."

Cian sneered. "He'll deceive you! He deceived my father and my people and then once he got what he wanted he burned them. All of them! Children!"

Conall held Cian's gaze as he said, "Cian, I do not doubt a word that you say. I don't trust him, nor any of the Gods. But I did want to hear what he had to say. Whether I believe a word of it is another story."

Cian leaned back in his chair, relieved. Conall said, "Artaius says that Lir and a few of the very powerful Gods are the ones that have pressed for the opening of hell, so that the demons may destroy everyone, in order to return back to the Creator."

He turned to Emrys. "You were right on that."

Conall leaned back in his chair and propped his feet on the table. "Artaius says that he and most of the lesser Gods fear that the Creator will exert his wrath, turning them into demons because of their involvement in this. That the Creator will not allow them into his realm because they had a hand in the destruction of this realm. He claims that they are playing along, appeasing Lir and the others but are really working to try to stop them, and have been working for centuries to come up with a contingency plan. Which is why he created vampires and hellhounds in the first place. To battle the demons. If the demons don't destroy all of human life while the realms are aligned, then the Gods cannot leave. It's also why he didn't destroy us, or the Fomoire. He was supposed to. He put us to sleep in case he needed us in the future. The other Gods were tricked by that. He was forced to annihilate the Fomoire. He knew of Cian and his people but let them survive, hoping they would go into hiding, but also binding them from reproducing just in case."

"Do you believe any of this?" Emrys asked.

Conall removed his feet from the table and leaned forward. "It doesn't matter whether I believe him or not. I don't trust him, and for every grain of truth he tells there are a hundred things he withholds. I do believe he's playing both sides and hedging his bets. That has always been his way. He's out for himself. I will work alongside him as long as it serves my purpose and my goals. We cannot have a realm without Gods. But we don't have to have a realm with Artaius in it, either."

Cian, Emrys and I all relaxed, Conall hadn't lost his mind and began trusting Artaius.

Conall stood and leaned on the table. "You've been caught up. Cian, you are now King of the Fomoire, correct?"

Cian nodded.

Conall extended his hand. "My brother, can we count on your alliance in this war?"

Cian grasped the King's hand and then they embraced as our old customs would have it.

Emrys and I stood, and Conall addressed us all, "Whatever plan we develop, we keep our true plan confined to our people. No half druids, no vamps or hounds. We will determine the best course of action and all have input on how we do it."

Conall placed his hands on my shoulder and kissed my cheek. "Welcome home, my Queen. Glad you're back."

He started to leave. "Morrigan, can you show Cian to a room? I believe the room next to yours is free. We'll make arrangements for his people to come stay here. The Knights are no longer Knights, and as hellhounds, are not welcome."

"Yes, my King," I replied.

Emrys, Cian and I walked towards our rooms. Cian would reside next to me and Emrys had the room across from mine. I felt a bond with these two like I had with no other. Kindred spirits.

We stopped in front of my room and I pointed to the door next to mine. "Cian, that's your room. It should be well stocked."

He nodded. I opened my door and grabbed each of their hands and pulled them in, shutting the door behind me.

We sat on my floor in a circle. Nobody said anything for several breaths.

"So your ex-boyfriend is now a hellhound," Cian began. "Guess that makes the odds low you'll be reconciling?"

We shared genuine laughter. The craziness of the past few days componded with the absurdity of the last hour was released.

"Either of you tired?" Emrys asked.

We shook our heads.

Emrys gave us his biggest ornery smile—the one I knew all too well. "Good. This realm is literally headed for Hell and we need a plan. No offense Morrigan, but running in and kicking ass isn't the best plan this time."

"None taken," I said giddily. I was made for this. The look on Cian's face told me he was up for it as well.

"Well then my friends," Emrys began, "let's begin planning something that they will never see coming."

NOTE FROM THE AUTHOR:

Reviews are always welcomed and appreciated. Please take the time to leave a quick one. And remember... I think you are smart and beautiful.

Ready to find out when the next book in this new series is released? Sign up for my newsletter and I promise to keep you in the loop!

You can also find more information at:
www.namontgomery.com

Made in the USA
Middletown, DE
17 November 2021

52762315R00099